DEATH AS A WAY OF LIFE

FRANCISCO AYALA

DEATH
AS A WAY
OF
LIFE

Translated from the Spanish by Joan MacLean

THE MACMILLAN COMPANY, NEW YORK

First Printing

The Macmillan Company, New York
Collier-Macmillan Canada Ltd., Toronto, Ontario

Library of Congress catalog card number: 64-12270

Printed in the United States of America

DEATH AS A WAY OF LIFE

CHAPTER

1

++++++++++++++++++++++++++++

Today we are too accustomed to seeing in the movies revolutions, wars, muggings, and mob scenes—all the spectacles of violence, in short, in which the human beast roars; but I think that one who has seen them only in the movies can ill imagine the astonishing simplicity with which, in reality, they unfold when it is a man's bad luck, as it is mine at the moment, actually to be a eyewitness. With the passing of time, occurrences of that sort doubtless will be the wonder of oncoming generations, and the man who has lived through them will pass for a hero for no other reason than that he survived. For my part, I hereby renounce all such glory and turn to the self-imposed task of unfolding this narrative in the bare bones of the simple truth. Here I am, in the eye of the hurricane, permanently confined to my wheelchair, an onlooker at such great and cruel upheavals, and until now no one has bothered about me. If my physical incapacity continues to serve me in good stead, if by some chance

[1]

it has not yet occurred to any blackguard to amuse himself at the expense of this wretched cripple or to shove him into the grotesque dance of death, it is quite probable that we may reach the end of this tale and that I may complete it. For it must have an end, and someone is going to have to tell it.

Meanwhile, I am kept alive by my insignificance. Who is going to trouble himself about me? I have time enough and more, and the tranquility to observe, inquire, find out, make sure of everything, and even to put together a set of files. Yes, I can assemble the papers that must serve as the valid documentary foundation for the history of this turbulent period. Of course, I have no intention of bragging about my services or of claiming any special merit for my dedication to collecting and compiling them; in what better way could I employ my time, after all? I come from a learned family and, in addition to that, I have been stuck in this wheelchair since the long-ago days of my adolescence. This sedentary task falls to me by right, even while people are doing their best to kill one another. To each his own, I say, and there is no vainglory in saying it; quite the contrary. To be sure, I realize fully that my condition would not be a great impediment to a man who enjoyed taking part in the upheavals of his time, all the better if he chanced to be blessed with a gift for politics—that goes without saying. Not so long ago, we had before us an example and a model for active paralytics in the person of Roosevelt. But we don't need to look that high. What about old Olóriz, crippled, by now no less handicapped than I, and half addled by senility to boot? Isn't he, in his fashion, today directing with his quaking hand the horrible saraband we are dancing? Isn't he the one passing out death sentences under the pretext of safeguarding the public welfare, ordering interrogations, and dispensing torture—in a word, manipulating the strings of all the puppets from his corner? He is, though it may seem incredible.

But I, on the contrary, poor thing that I am, who never have felt the itch of such desires, have done and am doing all I can to exploit my infirmity, to buttress my reputation as a passive reader and writer, even to the point of making myself appear

in the eyes of others that *rara avis,* that peculiar creature they
see in me, a kind of ludicrous owl with a powerful torso and
useless feet. Let them! They're the ones who are doing the fighting; they're struggling; they're clawing one another to death;
they're behaving like prima donnas driven by waves of blind
passion. Yet, when all is said and done, who can say that it may
not be my name, the name of Luis Pinedo, the insignificant
Little Pinedo, that will be famous, that will lead all the rest
because his one merit was to have saved from destruction and
oblivion these documents which no one recognizes as important
now, and to which no one pays any heed? Meanwhile, I keep
quietly assembling them so that when the time is ripe, I can
write up the present happenings. And, strangely enough, events
themselves have taken charge of bringing them, carried by their
own current, into my hands. Obviously, if several of the legations
had not been attacked by mobs, the fragments I now own, from
the archives scattered by the wind, never would have come into
my possession. If the Convent of Santa Rosa had not been broken
up, if its abbess had not sought a brief, shaky, and ephemeral
refuge in the Spanish legation, later sacked by a mob of mad-
men, I would not have in my keeping the bundle of letters and
rough drafts that occupy my files. I have succeeded in getting
together and classifying against the moment an ample store
of such papers—and some of them are very piquant, to be
sure.

Indeed, they are of all kinds, such as to suit all tastes; but
I must say that none of them is so precious to me or so unexpectedly revealing as the memoirs skillfully compiled in secret
day after day, on paper bearing the stamp of the presidency,
with unbelievable meticulousness and something of a good hand
for literature, by the obscure, troubled, and bold participant
who was to unleash the tragic events, only to become their first
victim straightaway: Private Secretary Tadeo Requena. The importance of certain keys to the puzzle contained in these long,
sometimes irrelevant reports may easily be imagined. They constitute a kind of autobiography of this brutal gray eminence
who, from his secondary level, played such an active role in

everything—a document of such importance that his script ought to be the keystone of any historical structure erected in the future.

I cannot pretend not to be fascinated by the prospect of myself being the architect of that impressive structure, always provided that we can reach port safely. The work is rewarding; it is well worth the effort, and I have a presentiment that it has been held in reserve for me. For the time being, I shall gain time by applying myself to the preliminary work of collating the data and organizing the materials, tracing the scattered sources, and outlining a commentary or two, a footnote or a glossary that will serve to pull it together, relate one event to another, filter out the facts, and establish the true weight and actual meaning of each event. In this way, I can quiet my anxiety, fill up my hours, and leave behind here, should luck desert me before the job is done, a rough draft—somewhat chaotic, yes, but, whatever happens, useful. I might even say indispensable, for in this blessed country of ours the memory of all things, the good as well as the bad, is soon lost. And this is not our least failing, if the truth be known; we live for the day, with no recollection of the past and no concern for the future, given over to a fatalism that wafts us from lethargy to frenzy, only, after each convulsion, to drop us, individually as well as collectively, back into lassitude. Perhaps that results from a supposition that nothing that happens or can happen here is real.

If you will forgive the digression, it cannot be denied, either, that our country does not count for much in the world; we ourselves hold it in low esteem; beneath all our lip service to it, we despise it, and we may as well admit it. Indeed, we are ashamed of it. But, whether or not we love it, the fact remains that we are dealing with a small country—too small, a poor corner of the tropics, isolated, lost among what, with patent hyperbole, we call "the great neighboring powers"—and, as if that were not enough, shut in behind that strip of land which constricts, strangles, and chokes us, that sort of free port here, an old pirates' nest, today a commercial emporium, which the

Dutch have been able to hold onto by who knows what miracle of shrewdness, of Providence, or of pure chance. Not one of those three factors has operated in our favor, on the contrary, with the result that nothing can be undertaken seriously or even be worth the effort in this unlucky little patch of ground— so we think or, rather, feel without going so far as to think. . . But then, I sometimes ask myself: does the size of a country have so very much to do with the memorable quality of what takes place in it? We have adopted the habit of consoling ourselves for the smallness of our country by comparing it to the Athens of Pericles and the Italian city-states of the Renaissance (this is a favorite argument that no one ever has rebutted; on the contrary, it is adduced over and over again, with indefatigable emphasis and repetition in our press, our radio, and courts). And, be that as it may, no one can deny that human beings live and struggle, gamble with their lives and lose them, and die, whether greatly or meanly, be their country minuscule or a giant empire. Each man has worth of his own, for what he is, for what he does and what he deserves, even though he may be reduced to playing his part within the frame of a little republic half asleep in the American wilderness.

I cherish the hope, therefore, that, descended as I am from a long line of famous learned men who were the glory and the admiration of this country in less unhappy days, I may find that the lofty mission of dealing out historical justice in a book has been reserved for me, and that it may also serve the dual purpose of a warning to generations to come and a permanent guide to these debased people, who must regain their old-time dignity someday, even though today they have been brought low through their own fault, though not so low as to be beyond reclaiming. As soon as the wave of violence, disaster, murder, robbery, arson, and all the other outrages that have afflicted our country since the death of President Bocanegra shall have subsided, I intend to apply myself to that task. And let me say in passing that in view of what has happened, I do not know whether his name should live in infamy, as many of us think, or whether it should be enshrined and mourned as the frustrated hope and ill-fated remedy for our country. At the moment, arranging my papers and my ideas, I am going ahead with the work, and I am laying out this sketch as a forerunner to the definitive book that I am promising myself to write later. While all around me everyone is brandishing the long knife or the machete, not to say the pistol, I shall be wielding my pen with no less bloodthirsty enjoyment.

CHAPTER

2

✦✦✦✦✦✦✦✦✦✦✦✦✦✦✦✦✦✦✦✦✦✦✦✦✦✦✦

Now I understand why the movies, literature, and historical accounts, even the word-of-mouth tales that are passed down to their grandchildren by eyewitnesses to events like these, always leave a false impression of spinning, dizzy motion, although curiously enough, the horror of such periods actually lies in the slow motion, the snail's pace of events. An insatiable, tense expectancy controls the situation, stretching the minutes, the hours, the days, the weeks, and the months to intolerable length. Yet the man who is telling the story piles murder on arson, arson on rape, rape on robbery, without meaning to, and so everything agglomerates, whirls, and is pressed together in very concentrated form, whereas he would be more accurate if he said that as matters actually developed, in reality, there were no such mobs or mob scenes, no such violent commotions, whirling action, or marching or trampling feet.

Instead it simply happens that perhaps one morning, as a man has just finished shaving, someone, another boarder in the same *pension,* comes to tell him with natural enough excitement that President Bocanegra has been found dead at the dawn of the morning after an official social function in the palace. Of course, conjecture is born immediately, and it is taken for granted that he must have suffered a heart attack, for it had always been feared—or so the envious and guilt-tinged slander ran—that his alcoholic and other excesses would lead to a sudden death like that. But not until later, when we were seated around the table at coffee time, would we come to find out (although in a still somewhat confused version shaped by a rumor which the remainder of the day would confirm) the sensational news that His Excellency had been murdered, and by none other than his own private secretary, young Tadeo Requena, whom he had taken under his wing. Suspicions of bedroom imbroglios might very well arise from that, and it might be inferred that on this very morning, the killer had . . . *et cetera.*

The news came slowly and in small bits. The few drops that fell were not enough to quench—on the contrary they increased —our thirst for information. From now on any amount whatever will seem only a drop. Everyone is concocting stories, spinning yarns, lying, leaving to the imagination the task of satisfying with some dubious morsel a curiosity already highly stimulated by the certainty that things are going to continue happening, and always from the shadows. Everyone was resenting his own need for sleep, and there were always plenty of people who would go out at all hours of the night, perhaps to look around and sniff out the victims whom daylight would punctually disclose, if not to lend a hand to the violence. Many a hand might tremble, though the informer's voice would not; and many a man committed his own murders on a breath or with a look that cast the shadow of suspicion.

Then came the gloating over the grisly details, the astonishment and speculation over the so-called warning examples. Chino López was found hanged head down from a tree in the dead-end San José Bendito road. When it was seen that his mouth had been stoppered with his own testicles, shoved between his

rotten teeth, who would not remember his sinister and celebrated skill as a professional gelder? Who would not speak the
name of the late Senator Rosales, his most famous "patient"?
Who would not guess, also, that what had cost that fool José
Lino his skin (may God forgive him) had been his arrogant
and endless series of shots on the billiard table in the Great
Aurora Café? What else could it be! And that the Galician, Rodríguez, had paid for his pedantic language in the columns of
El Comercio with his skin?

Two Spanish journalists had been hired as editors of that
great local newspaper, and it would seem that both of them had
become the victims of their own insolence. Many people had
sworn to get one of them, Camarasa, ever since about a year
ago, when he had published that famous and foolhardy article
on "How A Nation Is Made." It kicked up such a dust storm
that, given the opportunity offered by our current circumstances,
it sealed his death warrant. For a man to lose his life only because he had tried to be witty is just about the ultimate. But
that joke of his did have a political point, after all, and a fairly
sharp one upon analysis. When it came to the Galician, Rodríguez, however, with his schoolteacher-ish back-patting, or the
innocent boasting of poor José Lino, no one could use politics
as a pretext. In any case, as the author of his death was amusing himself by rubbing out that half-jesting wit, nothing could
have been farther from his mind than that he himself would
be forced to pay a high price for it before long. Camarasa was
an Andalusian refugee, somewhat sardonic and incapable of
holding his tongue or his pen, but when all was said and done,
he was not a bad sort.

True, that mysterious factor in human life which we call
luck can be seen operating more boldly and crudely on the
roulette wheel of such turbulent periods as this one. Every man's
good or bad luck comes up then through the most astonishing
combinations of chance. Yet in some cases almost a miracle
would have been needed to swerve a fate so perfectly foreseeable
under the circumstances as that of our luckless First Lady of
the Republic, the ineffable Doña Concha, through whose arms

hundreds had passed, willingly perhaps, there in the pigsty prison of the Immaculate Lady (euphemistically so designated by the public with a wink) until a sadistic cretin put a stop to the popular amusement by smashing her skull. The famous matron had wrought such a regrettable end for herself by her conduct, and there were those who could bring themselves to consider it a well-deserved punishment. They claimed that no one can display her bosom to an entire people for years and years with impunity—in photographs, in newsreels, and on television. Publicity can be a two-edged sword.

But there is something that no one knows yet, and it is one of the secrets that I am going to reveal to the world. To wit: that the lady had indeed earned her dreadful end, and not by anything venial. No, nothing so venial as her blameworthy habit of deliberately titillating *urbe et orbi* with her fascinating balloon breasts. Her mortal sin was her criminal manipulation of those who had given her God knows what unfortunate hankerings for the role of a Shakespearian heroine. All that may readily be inferred from the memoirs of Tadeo Requena, and must be duly set forth and documented at the proper point in these notes.

CHAPTER

3

++++++++++++++++++++++++++

This world is a fine surprise package; what memorabilia are to be found inside it! Who could have guessed? Few things escape my observation in this obscure Athens of the American tropics. Brought down by my infirmity to the role of a mere spectator from my seat in the theater, I see, perceive, and understand what passes unnoticed before almost anyone else. Those are the compensations granted to a cripple by his view from a wheelchair. Does anyone ever stop to think that a mouse, peering out from his hole, or a canary in its cage, may be noticing, unnoticed, everything that people say and do? I have traveled farther and seen more than those who were pushing and shoving and rushing hither and thither while I sat quietly either in the corner of a café watching others come and go or, perhaps, installed behind the billiard players who showed me the seat of their pants as they leaned over to line up their shots with painstaking care. But for all that, I must confess that the young secretary, Tadeo Requena, fooled me completely. The mouse and the canary failed me there. Finding his memoirs was such a surprise to me that I have not recovered from it yet.

How was it that that gray eminence—silent, unquestionably intelligent, but brutal and, above all, cold as a lizard and utterly despicable—that that type of unpolished opportunist, that flawless example of the rampant miscegenation that is devastating our country today, came to be in the secret places of his self a fine gentleman endowed with literary inclinations, no less? And not only that, but an implacable critic of the society surrounding him, too; a little fellow quite capable of taking out his disgruntlements under the guise of irony; a man who became, in the end, a member of the class of individualists who permit themselves the eccentricity, permissible only in invalids, of employing their leisure time in scribbling and doodling on reams of paper for the sheer joy of informing on themselves, betraying and selling themselves? Was he like me, after all, an animal of the same breed as mine; I mean, a brother under the skin? If that stack of papers had been swept out with the trash instead of falling by pure chance into my hands, how much a matter of course it would have been in times such as these, with disorder regnant everywhere, to dismiss Tadeo Requena with a good-bye forever! His little-known name would have been buried along with his bullet-torn body, and with him a portion of contemporary history, curious and instructive, even to some degree monitory to us at least, though unimportant to the rest of the world. For nothing is more certain than that these memoirs can by rights be given pride of place in the series of documents I am collecting and am planning to present here in essence as the basis for my future book.

Of course, a good many things in the memoirs have no bearing on the case, or sometimes vitiate what is interesting in a mass of trivial or gratuitous details relevant only to the author himself and to his preoccupations; for the fellow was completely egocentric beneath that half-fierce, half-servile manner which had made him the president's watchdog. I am vowing to myself that I will omit from the manuscript or summarize everything that does not deal with the course of public life, even though I cannot resist reproducing right here and now, at the start, something of the story he tells concerning the beginnings of his good fortune and how he happened to come, or to be brought rather, to the capital (I almost said to court). And I still wonder why the young Tadeo failed to add to his design that precarious and hasty culture poured down his throat by Dr. Luisito Rosales, and which he doubtless swallowed greedily, however scornfully he might attempt to conceal it, so as to evoke at that point the illustrious comparisons with his strange destiny that History, with a capital H, could provide. Yes, indeed, it seems strange to me that, given his delusions of grandeur, he did not remind the world of the first flattering comparison that springs to mind: the famous and imperial Don John of Austria.

Requena, the private secretary, starts his memoirs with some general reflections or commonplaces concerning life and the unguessable quirks of fate—which is not a bad idea and offers proof of his literary instinct. "Inscrutable" is the pretentious word he uses again and again. He exclaims: "If only one could actually read the future!" This exclamation, this sigh, is the first phrase his pen traces, only to go on at once to lament that the portents Fate hands out, always blurred, frequently are bound to prove deceptive; that a man often starts something under the most favorable auspices, only to have everything turn out badly. Then, too, it may frequently happen that something that seemed to you a misfortune at first will take a turn for the best and prove to be a blessing, and thus come around in the end to confirm the initial portents, so that actually no one knows anything. Clearly, poor Tadeo Requena is writing an overture in that key and with a certain rhetorical dignity, to introduce the theme of the fabulous turn his fortunes took and to underline how much of what pertained to him held an element of the unexpected, of a dream that he could not believe in. "I was just a hapless ne'er-do-well then; less than a nobody, a nothing. More than once I have stepped down from my present position, not without some complacency, to renew my acquaintance with myself in that state of abandonment. I was not even conscious of my miserable state, God help me; I paid no heed to it whatsoever, for, after all, my luck was the same black lot as that of a great many others, of everyone," he explains.

The truth is that his somewhat rhetorical astonishment at the unexpected turns the world can take might have been much greater, and his ponderings might have turned very bitter, if an untimely death had not cut short the thread of his outspoken memoirs. Later events provided truly miraculous examples of some very apt and dramatic illustrations of his thesis. For example, who could have told President Bocanegra at the time he picked up this young Tadeo on his own initiative, educated him, and kept him at his side, that this youth would exercise such a disastrous influence over the flimsy structure of his power, over his terrible reputation, ruined at a single stroke? Perhaps the dying glance shot at his secretary by the supreme chief—his last look, for he already was in his mortal throes—had pinpointed in memory the date and the occasion when he had sent one of his trusted men, then Major and now Colonel Cortina, to the village of San Cosme to find the boy and bring him posthaste to the presidential presence. As for Tadeo himself, how could that poor devil have imagined that that very man, that very Pancho Cortina who fetched him from the village in fulfillment of orders from above, that Major Cortina who had been the object of his open admiration from the very beginning, would ultimately be the one to shoot him down like a dog, and thus write an epilogue to these memoirs, an epilogue written in blood with a pistol? At first glance he had looked like a messenger angel and guardian in the doorway. Yes, poor Tadeo Requena, you yourself could not know just how unforeseeable is the course of human existence, nor what unsullied truth envelops the phrases and the mannerisms with which you, as an enthusiastic man of letters, started off your memoirs.

After his exordium, which is not out of place or clumsy, though not original either, the author makes his entrance, stepping gracefully into straightforward narrative. The future private secretary begins now, without more ado, to tell the story of his life. He says, and I quote him verbatim: "I must have been somewhere around seventeen or eighteen years old at the time. I was a grown man, and I was good for nothing. But what could I do? There was no work to be had there. Like all the rest of the country, the village was napping; people talked slowly; they moved sluggishly; some of them had gone to the Dutch trading houses to work themselves to death; some who were luckier had managed to get to the United States, and once there, they stayed. I realized that some fine day before very long I too would have to get out and look for work; but for the time being I preferred not to think about anything, and I killed time by just staring around me, open-mouthed like an idiot. How could I ever have suspected, ever dreamed, what was in store for me? At that stage in my life, President Bocanegra meant little more to me than that mustached image with a ribbon worn diagonally across its chest which kept repeating itself on all the walls of the saloons, the bakery, the office of food supply, the school; that everlasting portrait, plus a remote aura of incontrovertible power compounded of the vaguest fears and hopes.

"Then, suddenly one day, as if by sleight of hand, I find myself being taken, unbelievably, to an interview with him. It must have been about two o'clock, or a little after, as I was sprawled in the shade, enduring the heat, with my back against the door of the warehouse—the property of Luna, the Galician —next to the square. Suddenly I could hear the roar of motorcycles—the police. I stretch out my neck; one, two outriders, and immediately following them a jeep, and inside the jeep, an officer. I went up to them slowly, like all the others, to look and listen out of curiosity. What the hell! I was the one they were looking for! When the officer stuck out his head and asked for Tadeo, Belén's Tadeo, all the grownups looked at me apprehensively and the little kids pointed me out with proud and officious fingers. Then one of the two guards took me by the arm, without a word of explanation, and shoved me into the car, next to the major.

" 'Don't be afraid,' he said with a laugh, his teeth very white beneath his very black mustache. He was trying to reassure me.

" 'I'm not scared,' I told him fiercely. But I was thinking at that very moment of Juancito Álvarez, only a year older than I, who had been picked up like that a short time before, together with two older men. What happened to them no one ever found out.

"My lot was destined to be quite different. The officer managed to instill confidence in me. He assured me that I was not heading for anything bad, but the contrary. He told me his name.

" 'I'm Major Francisco Cortina,' he said, making an effort to be friendly. For my part, I had not a glimmer of a clue. I kept thinking that, whatever it was, it would come out. That was my way of keeping my wits about me. After all, I thought, with poor people nothing is ever too good, but nothing is ever too bad, either. I set myself to watching the road. I had never been out of San Cosme before. We passed through several villages. I stared at them and the people stared at me as we went by like a shot.

"I shall never forget our entrance into the capital. I would have been glad if the jeep had not gone so fast then. It was just like in the movies. I had toured the streets of New York and Chicago with my eyes in the village movie theater. I knew Mexico City especially well; I had caught glimpses of Buenos Aires, Paris, and London. This city, although our capital, did not resemble any of them. But, on the other hand, it had the advantage of being real; it was here in the flesh, so to speak, and here I was, inside it. Our jeep passed like a scurrying mouse through street after street, until finally it found a hole for itself in a patio which, as I later learned, belonged to the National Palace, no less. And that very patio is the one I can look into from the window of my room now, with jeeps constantly coming and going, and hordes of guards arguing or indulging in horseplay. Major Cortina was a member of the household. He led me up stairways and along corridors, in the wake of his brightly polished jackboots and jingling spurs, to a room where he finally halted and told me to wait for him.

[16]

"There I was, there meaning here, for I'm almost certain that the room was this same outer office where I now have my desk. At that time it was furnished as a parlor, with a sofa, some armchairs, and some straight chairs. I sat down in a corner, and I don't know how long I had to wait. After a while I felt ravenously hungry, for I had probably not eaten more than a couple of bananas all day. At home I never wanted to eat whatever little there was because I did not like to be told afterward how lazy I was.

"I thought with displeasure of my old lady, of how grimy and grumbling she was, with a swarm of little pickaninnies hanging onto her skirts. When would she begin to miss me? Tomorrow? Never! People would already have gone to her with the news, and she would be all in an uproar. Why wouldn't they have brought her the story at once? Yes, of course they had. Apart from all the youngsters, Luna, the Galician, and others had seen the guards carry me off in the jeep. At the moment when that thought came into my mind, I remembered catching a sly, scoffing look from Luna out of the corner of my eye, a very Galician look, which I could not stop to interpret in all the confusion of the occasion, but which had stayed engraved on my mind all the while. Later on, with the passing of time, I realized that in fact no one in the village had been surprised or alarmed, and I realized that they had always taken me for a youngster destined to become a protegé of someone in high office. I sensed that when my own mother learned of it, she would remark with some rancor, 'It's about time they gave him a job, at least with the police.' And she would have gone on to prophesy bitterly, 'Of course he'll forget all about his people right away.' And the truth is, now that I think of it, I should have liked to do something for them. Some day when the kids are a little older, I'll have the chance to help them. So far I've had all I could do just to take care of myself. As for her, the poor woman, she is beyond my help now: she's been underground for about four years. Some day I shall have to go to the village cemetery and look for her grave so that I can have a handsome headstone put on it.

[17]

"But after all, what could I have expected from her? She did not even know where to look for me. She was living as if in a dream, where one goes through the most absurd situations unchanged. It may not seem possible, but after I had been caught up in that strange set of circumstances, fetched to that luxurious drawing room on wings, as it were, into a setting the like of which I had never seen, the only thing that I was bothered about was the hunger clawing like a cat inside my stomach. They had left me alone, but occasionally I could hear whispers in the distance or doors being slammed in other rooms. I hardly dared to move from the spot I was on, and I was beginning to set a time when I would get up and start walking away until someone should stop me. Then, suddenly I saw the door begin to open. . ."

That is how Tadeo Requena tells about his entrance into the presidential palace. He goes on to tell how, after such a long wait, he supped that night—like a savage, he says—and slept like a log among the bodyguards. Not until the following morning was well along did the new Segismundo, whose part he had begun to play, resume the vivid dream by being brought into the palace again and finally led into the august presence of Bocanegra. Under what circumstances? It will be more worthwhile to give the exact words of the person most involved. The manners and customs of the filthy dictator under whom we have suffered are depicted by him with a naïve naturalness, with an eloquence greater than the angry denunciations and reproaches addressed to him by his worst detractors.

"Major Cortina," Tadeo Requena goes on to say, "came in person to see me the next day and again he had me climb the marble staircases. 'Please come along with me, young man,' he said to me. I followed him through galleries and corridors, smudging the gleaming wood of the floors with my canvas sandals, to a place completely strange to me at the time, a room that I, poor ignoramus that I was, had never even dreamed of! In actual fact, that was the first time in my life that I had entered a bathroom, with its shining mosaic tiles and its extraordinary installations. Indeed I have never since seen anything that was larger or more sumptuous. It was what might really be called a salon, for a crowd of well-known luminaries were gathered there at that moment. Among them I recognized with astonishment and a kind of feeling of relief someone I know—Dr. Don Luisito Rosales, the brother of our late senator.

"I knew him, I say. Yes, I knew him as an ownerless dog may know the lord of the manor. How could I help knowing him? But my relief was idiotic, for he, on the other hand, had never taken any notice of me or even been aware of my existence, anymore than he would that of any other washerwoman's son who helps to pick up the laundry once or twice, meanwhile seizing his chance to glance furtively and admiringly into the interior of the big house. Nowadays that gentleman's house, or the Rosales mansion as we also used to call it, has been closed for some time, ever since the violent death of the senator. When that occurred, the family scattered; the widow went to New York with her children, and the brother, this same Don Luisito, settled shortly afterward in the capital and seldom returned to San Cosme, especially after his appointment as a cabinet officer in the government.

"Well, I can see myself now in that bathroom, among gentlemen who darted contemptuous glances at my shrinking presence as I entered on the major's coattails, yet never entirely withdrew their attention from that other luminary toward whom they were all looking up in anxious deference. That man, half hidden by the crowd, was President Bocanegra himself—I almost died of fright when I recognized him. Bocanegra in the flesh and spirit, with the demon-haunted eyes and the drooping moustaches, whom I had known so well by sight from his portrait in the saloon, though now without the band across his chest, of course. Indeed His Excellency, the one real leading light among that distinguished society, was seated, was perched on the toilet seat, or the sanitary fixture as I soon learned to call it, and was presiding over his dignitaries from that stool of honor.

"At that moment when I was being introduced in that fashion, being suddenly plumped down among that inner circle of the privileged, in a sanctuary where mere admittance implied the highest honor of state, hundreds and thousands of citizens would have envied me if they had known of my almost fabulous good fortune. I was to learn all this later, and Dr. Rosales himself was to be the one to teach me, as he taught me many and many another thing that has proved so useful to know in the time that has elapsed since. I owe the doctor my thanks for that, and I should be a most ill-bred man if I were to refuse him the gratitude I owe him, however harshly he administered his teachings, however much he wore me out by his dilly-dallying over needlessly prolix explanations instead of getting to the heart of the matter.

"As an example, the doctor judged that under the circumstances he was in duty bound to bore me with a long lecture apropos of this intimacy and familiarity, which our *caudillo* used to dole out with such a niggardly hand and which he condescended to extend to me from the very beginning. The lecture was delivered at the right moment, crammed with facts (perhaps invented by him for all I know) on the *levée*—the morning reception, as he went on to explain, held by the kings of France. This dissertation was further embellished with anecdotes only marginally related to the theme, such as the tale of the death of Sancho Somebody-or-Other of Castille, whom the traitor Bellidos spitted on his spear as the helpless monarch was voiding himself near an adobe wall. And as if that were not enough, he enlarged on the *arcana imperii* with very involved digressions—meanwhile leaning backward to hear himself better—concerning the chambers which, although they enclosed the potentate, isolated him at the same time and created a very rarefied atmosphere about him. I always used to try to winnow a strawstack of words and to get something useful out of it. I think I got it, and actually, modesty aside, this is more to the pupil's than the teacher's credit.

"But to turn back now to my story: as I was saying, I suddenly sighted Bocanegra, no less, in the middle of that tightly pressed gathering, to the utter confusion of the wretched rustic I was then. And I chanced to see him when he had already fastened his eyes on me. I nearly jumped out of my skin, but luckily I kept my head and managed to appear as cool as could be, so cool that I think I must have seemed even somewhat insolent. He addressed me from his throne (and that was the first time I had ever heard his harsh voice, strangely enhanced by soft, almost flexible modulations) .

" 'So this is Tadeo!' he exclaimed; then speaking directly to me, 'Come here, boy, come closer. . .' Now, and only now, the others considered themselves apprised of my presence, and they poured the chrism of their friendly glances over my lowly head; they even nudged me gently toward the *caudillo*. Mistrustful, incredulous, I heard talk then, somewhat sybilline in its phrasing, concerning plans, projects, and designs having to do with me. Out of that fog of words, I was able to make out that for the time being I was to be turned over to the good offices of the Minister of Public Instruction (that is to say, Dr. Rosales, then present) as well as to those of Major Pancho Cortina, who had brought me there. They were to watch over me and to look out, respectively, for my physical well-being and my spiritual development, and in the shortest possible time—understand? —they were to prepare me for whatever mission or position the president should assign to me. 'I want you to see you make him a little doctor of laws, without any delay, eh? Without a moment wasted'!"

CHAPTER

4

++++++++++++++++++++++++++

       "A little doctor of laws . . . without a moment wasted." That was Bocanegra. His conscientious private secretary-to-be began working on that portrait the very first day. This sharp yokel was to be turned into a doctor overnight, for no other reason than that it was the president's wish. Still, Bocanegra had grounds for that. Hadn't our famous old National University of San Felipe, carrying the dual title of royal and pontifical, humbled itself shortly before then by granting him, a superannuated former student who had flunked out, its highest and most prized honorary doctor's degree solely because it had become obvious that he had risen to power? A little doctor of laws . . . without a moment wasted! I, who had spent five years wheeling myself through those halls of learning, as my legs were of no use to me, in order to be entitled to call myself a lawyer, while this. . . A special case!

    And it goes without saying that the ineffable Luisito Rosales, to whom the wish of the Big Boss literally was law, not content with fitting the academic gown to those strapping shoulders almost before the fellow's first pair of shoes had come from the last, also took charge, most officiously, of teaching him some manners, polishing him, tutoring him, and making him, in a word, presentable by comparison with the gaggle of shysters who pullulate in the national offices. To top all that, he not only succeeded, but even managed to endow his pupil with a certain intellectual air, impressive at first glance, though the luxurious cloak of a superior culture, hastily thrown over him, sometimes failed to conceal the rags of his original indigence. These memoirs I'm using as source material bear witness to that preposterous combination of a princely education and academic short courses. The writing shows a good deal of literary vanity and an art that cannot be dismissed contemptuously, but its author did not always manage to avoid mistakes in spelling.

In all fairness we must recognize that the entire first portion of his writings (in which the young smalltown boy was working delightedly in the palace, giving full rein to the immense vanity that oozed from every pore in his hide, only muted, contained, or held in check from time to time by the no less insolent arrogance that was native to him and that, in him, resulted in an odd combination of insecurity and aplomb) turns out now to be of inestimable value. Tadeo Requena's personality could not be thanked for that, for the fellow was not, after all, as interesting as he imagined himself to be. The script has served mainly as a guide to a clear and accurate understanding of the genesis of the present upheavals: it goes deeply into the prehistory of the immediate past, which, by sheer accident, has come to reveal to us the obscure secretary and to lay bare his murderous deed—by that deed alone placing him at the center of historical events.

We can see through his memoirs how the monster was hatched, and we can trace the first, hidden stages of the infection that was to break out later in a raging fever. I myself, and most people like me, had no clear idea of the background of the fateful secretary whom everyone preferred not to take very seriously, despite the effective power he had got into his hands. Consequently, no one could have imagined what he was to unleash in the fullness of time by his one precipitate, headlong act. If memory serves, the first time I ever heard him mentioned was when it became known that Bocanegra had appointed him his private secretary. Surely there must have been talk about him in the Great Aurora Café and Billiard Hall, where I used to spend my afternoons, but I think that no one was quite sure whom they were talking about. The usual slanders that draw, dress, and season the commentaries on any news of the day were concentrated this time on the conjectured father-and-son relationship said to exist between the president and his brand-new protegé, whom no one there had known, but who as a matter of course was taken to be one of the many by-blows left behind him all over the country by that animal Bocanegra. To be sure, the matter failed to cause much of a stir, so that, for lack of other elements to introduce some exciting variations on the theme, the tittle-tattle soon subsided. Very likely it was true, after all.

Tadeo himself, too wary and too proud to admit openly what had doubtless been common gossip in the village of San Cosme too, shapes his memoirs in such a way as to let the moot question be glimpsed in several passages, and particularly in the one where he refers to the tasteless joke once played on him by the Galician, Luna, even though he has to drag it in more or less by the hair of its head. Luna, owner of the grocery store on the square, had called out to him from behind the show window, saying, "What are you doing here, Tadeo? You, boy, when your moustache grows, all you have to do is look a little pompous and even the soldiers will salute you as they go by." Be that as it may, the question was of no importance whatsoever, and people did not bother their heads very much about the new private secretary. His appointment could not have been very much of a shock to anyone. It was just one of the Big Boss's whims, a run-of-the-mill appointment, no different from any other he might have made to the same post. Every man seeks his collaborators and his henchmen among his own kind, and though Bocanegra had come from a good family, his back-alley tastes were well known, and that incorrigible proclivity of his for associating with the rabble gave them an ugly cast.

So, as I say, no one thought the matter very important, not even the newspapers, which make their living by blowing up any bit of news. They published an item characterizing Dr. Tadeo Requena as "one of our promising young men . . . a distinguished lawyer" and a "most brilliant example of the new generation that is entering the public arena with hearts filled with a passionate hope, and to whom our illustrious leader, the President of the Republic, always on the alert for the future good of our country, is opening broad channels through which, little by little, they may assume the responsibilities of leadership and the functions of the civil government." But it is plain that all this was said without departing from the routine puff by officialdom.

On only one occasion did I hear—and then it came, of course, from the lips of Camarasa, that poor, loquacious Camarasa who has come to such a bad end—only once, I say, did I hear the appointment of Requena interpreted as something highly, even transcendentally significant. According to him, the appointment of the new private secretary, plus the dictator's manifest intention of taking him under his wing, indicated that the *caudillo* had carefully laid plans for starting his government on a new tack . . . I do not know why Camarasa took it upon himself to come to me and enlarge upon the theme. Perhaps it was because he already was somewhat far gone in drink when he entered the café, and because he found no one else there but José Lino, the dimwit with whom he could not exchange two consecutive words on any subject.

In any case, after sweeping the place with a bored glance, he came over and let himself down beside my wheelchair so as to have another cognac at my side. He patted me on the back, called me Little Pinedo with his usual familiarity, and then began at once to display his uncontrollable fluency with words. He went from one subject to another, and finally favored me by offering a theory with reference to the Bocanegran power which he had fabricated full-blown. He explained that public preachments and popular agitation had been the principal expedients of this demagogue, and that his easy but infallible gambit consisted—as who could forget?—of gathering together as many subjects and *leitmotifs* as he needed to cause the old wounds of the poor to ache, however contradictory those gambits might be. He would brandish those injuries while he scattered indiscriminate, fearless, and irrelevant promises to the four winds.

"Isn't that so?" Camarasa asked me, and I agreed. There was nothing new to me or to anyone else in that, of course. It was an old twice-told tale to everyone. But Camarasa had to review "past history" in order to compose his picture. That done, he went ahead: "He rose to power by means of a single shrewd stroke (and a clever one, by God, for the fellow's sharper than the serpent's tooth; you can't take that away from him). And, once risen to power, thanks to carelessness, surprise, and the confusion among the upper classes, whom his outcries had terrorized, the new president again cheated his own people by electing to satisfy his baseless resentments at a banquet of refined and hypocritical reprisals, cold-blooded humiliations, taunts, all the more irritating for being petty, and—what is truly unbearable—by granting everything to the mob instead of settling disputes realistically as might have been expected, and establishing himself as the head man . . ."

According to Camarasa, who was explaining with enjoyment all that had happened, that first phase of Bocanegra's government had reached its climax and culminated in the assassination of Senator Rosales, the only member of the old families who had been capable of seriously disquieting the dictator. Once that obstacle had been removed, his course was set, and the subsequent "capitulation and surrender" of the victim's brother, the unlucky Luisito Rosales, in accepting, to the general scandal and dismay, the offer of the portfolio of Public Instruction offered him by Bocanegra, had been only the patent symbol of a melancholy fate. With that move, an entire period of the national history came to a close. From then on—at this point Camarasa's little eyes, filled with enthusiasm at his own perspicuity, gleamed with intelligence and alcoholic excitement—from then on the dictator, with insuperable power in his hands, set about preparing for himself—and I would live to see it—a Pharaoh-like edifice, and he would sacrifice the very slaves upon whom he originally had depended, but whose support he no longer needed for any purpose whatsoever.

"You'll see, Pinedito, that I'm not kidding myself about this. His former lenience toward the shorn sheep's mischief will change into implacable repressions now, until no one will dare to make a move. I have to laugh when I think of the simpletons who talk about his honesty as an administrator only because they can see that he lives modestly at the apex of power. Why should he take anything from the treasury's coffers as long as he thinks it will be all his as soon as he has converted the state into his private estate?"

Camarasa was laughing, sparkling with malice. "But true or false, what does all that have to do with the appointment of a new private secretary? Will you tell me that? Well, son, it's plain enough that Bocanegra (Black Mouth) or Almanegra (Black Soul) was in dire need of such types as this Tadeo Requena so that he could use them to carry out his plan of operations. He had to have men who were his own creatures, body and soul—omnipotent as long as they're under his wing, dead rats in the street. Own son of his or not, that particular nobody was made to order. He can't laugh off the fact that the dictator plucked him out of the grimmest poverty, to metamorphose him into his faithful dog, his good right hand (or perhaps his left, for after all, the left hand must never know what the right hand doth, according to the Biblical maxim for governing well) ."

Hadn't I noticed too, Camarasa asked, how Pancho Cortina, for his part, is beginning to look like a rising star? "Another young man without any links to the old families, the son of a Spaniard who died too soon to have been able to make his fortune." Pancho had been promoted from a mere policeman to the position of general factotum in the State Security Administration, even though his commission as major barely was out of the oven. "Watch out for that young scamp, too. Now that

[28]

he has a hand in the police force, it wouldn't surprise me at all if we were to see that branch develop at the expense of the regular army. It would have been no easy trick to suddenly oust the old colonels and the drunken generals who had become so much dead weight in the armed forces. They would have turned out to be unmanageable, owing to their inertia and their vices stemming from idleness, their pretensions, and their thousands of cunning tricks. No, this petty Central American dictator," the Spaniard Camarasa went on to remark in a scornful tone, "was not carrying his lesson from Hitler in a leaking pail."

He was keeping a fixed stare on me as he licked the last drop of cognac from his wet lips. What did I have to say about all this, eh? Of course I hadn't a word to say. I was listening, glancing around me apprehensively all the while, for the rascal had lost control of himself, and I could have been compromised in the stupidest possible way.

Yes, poor Camarasa was very imprudent indeed, as later events were to prove. As a matter of fact, he could have come to no other end than the one he came to, however lamentable that was. Each man is the author of his own fate; each is responsible, first and last, for whatever happens to him. No one can be as careless as Camarasa was with impunity. It cannot be denied that the man had a keen nose for news, as he showed in his interpretations and prophecies of the course of national politics; and in view of certain details it might even be said that he was able to see beneath the surface—although in what had to do with the death of Senator Rosales, no one needed the eyes of a lynx to foresee the consequences of that crime, which no one could fail to impute to President Bocanegra through either commission or omission. Lucas Rosales had been carrying on a campaign of violent opposition, not only from his seat in the senate, but also by making use of every means at his command—few enough to be sure—and especially by enlisting the support of the clergy, who lent his cause the subtle, very powerful resources of the pulpit and the confessional. Behind the scenes of that campaign some sort of conjurer's trick readily could be conjectured, some mighty blow to the preparation of which the upper echelons of the army had committed themselves actively, body and soul. So that when the newspapers published in big red headlines the news that the senator from the province of Tucaití, Don Lucas Rosales, had been shot down as he was climbing the steps to the capitol to officiate at a meeting of the senate, no one could fail to think of the "overwhelming impulse" that the aggressors undoubtedly had obeyed.

At this point I turn to an extract from a copy of the circumspect report on this event which the Spanish minister accredited to our old capital city sent to his chief in Madrid. It forms a part of the legacy of documents which, thanks to my tenacity and the help given me this time by a veritable congeries of circumstances, I have succeeded in collecting because of the attack on the legation, and which I am keeping neatly filed in my set of folders. These diplomatic reports have proven invaluable to me in reconstructing the developments of the situation, for—as will be clear to everyone—they afford me the point of view of a foreign observer, who, even though somewhat confused by a mass of prejudices, does exploit the advantages of a very exceptional position and is able to see things as an outsider.

The text relative to the assassination of Senator Rosales is particularly clear, extensive, and serious. This—copied word for word—is what it says:

"My Dear Excellency: It is my duty today to report to Your Excellency on events that are serious to a degree that, unless I am mistaken, may mark a critical point in the process of decomposition (or, if you prefer, of revolutionary change, as some people put it) to which this country has been subjected. Senator Lucas Rosales, the undisputed leader of the opposition forces, was shot to death as he was making his way to the door of the senate at three o'clock yesterday afternoon. The unidentified gunmen had hidden themselves behind one side of the framework of the staircase leading to the capitol building, where they could empty their weapons into him at no risk whatsoever and then get safely away to a hideout. The spot for the attempt was very well chosen, for once the senator had left his automobile, he had to climb the broad stairway to reach the senate floor. The staircase therefore provided a blind from which the hunters could not miss. People have asked one another how the assassins could have managed to get into such a place, calmly lie in wait there, and disappear without a trace once their deed was done.

"The death of Señor Rosales immediately aroused a great commotion, gave rise to a state of general anxiety, and set everyone into motion, some in the grip of panic, others made bold, arrogant, and threatening, but one and all highly excited. None of the outrages of the past months has had such repercussions as this one promises, as indeed it already is beginning to produce, owing as much to the personality of the victim as to the circumstances surrounding the event.

"Don Lucas Rosales, the murdered senator, was the real hope and the leader of the forces of order, so cruelly castigated by the course of action followed by the present regime. He had arrived at that position only a short time ago by virtue of his noteworthy traits of character, his outstanding work in the emergency, and his social eminence. He commanded, so to speak, not only his own village of San Cosme and all the surrounding country, but the entire province of Tucaití as well, the one section of the country, as perhaps Your Excellency may recall, that at the time of the elections was capable of holding out successfully against the attacks of the mad demagogues directed by Antón Bocanegra, today the President of the Republic, and even then the well-known and feared 'Father of the Poor,' as he was pleased to call himself before he had tasted the honors enjoyed by a head of state.

"I realize, Your Excellency, that with so many and varied matters to claim your attention, you cannot bear in mind the details of the local situation in every Central American country, and for that reason, I shall permit myself to remind you that most of the benches in both the lower house and the senate have been in the control of President Bocanegra ever since he won a series of elections through terrorism. He has yielded to the pressure of the mobs and has not hesitated to turn them loose upon this hapless country for the purpose of terrorizing it. They have destroyed everything to their grotesque and ominous cry of

'Long live the FP' (an abbreviation of 'Father of the Poor'). In view of those circumstances, Senator Rosales, who until then, and indeed throughout his life, had devoted himself solely to administering his inheritance, like so many other great landowners, and whose only contacts with politics and government had been those normal and proper to a man in his position, came to the conclusion that he was in duty bound to enter the lists and take an active part in public affairs. Immediately thereafter he began to gravitate naturally toward leadership, and did in fact become a leader. During his last days, he had grown enormously in stature, for whereas the other landowners felt frustrated, lost, and utterly routed, he kept a cool head. Above all, he hit upon a means for constructing a strategy to fight Bocanegrism with the object of extricating his country from anarchy. According to what is contained in one of the press clippings that I had the pleasure of sending Your Excellency as an appendix to one of my earlier reports, wherein I was dealing, I feel sure, with some article transparently inspired from the top, Senator Rosales was in effect imputed to be the moving force behind the abortive military plot uncovered months ago. (In my opinion, whatever the matter I was discussing may have been, that imputation was not entirely baseless.) You may judge from this the impact that the news of his assassination has had on both sides. Suffice it to say (and Your Excellency will forgive me for adducing such trivia by way of illustration) that the radio announcer from whom I heard the news immediately after the crime had been committed, proclaimed it in a trembling voice, stumbling over his words.

"I have assembled this report in order that Your Excellency may the better form a judgment on the basis of the attitude of the press, less intense now, but more thoughtful. The popular conviction that this bloody deed is invested with a decisive character may be inferred from the clippings. Now the existing tension is bound to be resolved, one way or another. And, pending further opinion, I am afraid that, far from yielding a healthy reaction, highly improbable at the moment, this event may serve only to accentuate the present evils and to make them irreparable. The most sensible and experienced members of the diplomatic corps share this impression with me. More than that, it is thought that the suppression of Senator Rosales was not decreed without a careful previous examination of the pros and cons. In any case, this is not a question of a sporadic act that can be laid to irresponsible men. It may be worth-while to point out, apropos of that, that for several days now strange rumors have been circulating concerning the alleged atrocity that a group of the senator's field hands, farm workers, or day laborers had planned to perpetrate upon him by subjecting him in broad daylight to a brutal surgical operation obviously intended to deprive him of any basis for boasting from then on of his masculinity. I must warn Your Excellency parenthetically that such things are not unthinkable in the social environment of these barbarous American rural areas. I think, however, that the rumor was floated for the sole purpose of besmirching in the minds of the rabble the good name of a powerful and formidable political enemy. However that may be, it points up the existence of aggressive designs, in view of which it would not be overly bold to characterize yesterday's deed as fully premeditated. All that is lacking now is to see what the investigation to be opened at the order of the presiding officer of the senate will amount to. As he considered the matter to lie within the purview of the legislative body, he has made it the official business of the commander of the guard. No arrests whatever have been made up to now, as far as I know.

"I shall keep Your Excellency abreast of everything that happens from now on through further reports to come."

CHAPTER

5

✦✦✦✦✦✦✦✦✦✦✦✦✦✦✦✦✦✦✦✦✦✦✦✦

The Minister Plenipotentiary of Spain, a conscientious official and nobody's fool, as anyone can see, reports on the death of Senator Rosales in those terms to his superiors in rank. Clearly, he was not far off the mark in his evaluation of the consequences of the episode, and time has operated to prove him right. I should have been keenly interested to learn his reaction to the fact that the brother of the victim should accept a minister's portfolio only a few months after his grievous loss and swear allegiance to the man whom everyone, openly or covertly, was naming as the moral author of the assassination. But unfortunately, my incomplete file of documents lacks a copy of the report that deals with it—provided that there was such a report, as I am certain there was.

As for the comments from all sides that were made here in our immediate environs concerning the conduct of this Luisito Rosales, I need no report from anyone. An ample stock of them already had come to my ears, tailored to every taste and de-livered in every tone, from the indignant to the disrespectful, from the amused to the ironic. A newspaperman was quick to compose a bit of doggerel. The Galician, Rodríguez, composed a series of satirical verses, far from good, and full of the usual non-sense, but brimming over with pungent ironies. Included among them was a passing swipe at my uncle, General Malagarriga, a slap that was basically unfair even though my uncle had been the first to serve the FP, the Father of the Poor, by accepting the portfolio of Minister of War, as the Galician said. I myself had felt obliged to disapprove of that act at the time. But the case of my poor uncle Antenor was not colored by those peculiarly ag-gravating circumstances which made the case of Rosales un-forgivable. The fact is that if Bocanegra's intention in appoint-ing him a member of his cabinet (I am referring now to Luisito Rosales) had been to discredit and blacken the name of that old and illustrious family for all time after ruining them, then no one can doubt that he accomplished his generally supposed intention *in excelsis*. The catcalls from decent people were deaf-ening, the more so in many cases because the breath of envy was blowing the fire of moral indignation into flames.

In contrast, I was struck by a paragraph I happened to come across in Tadeo Requena's memoirs in which he not only ex-cuses in passing the loudly decried conduct of his teacher, but even goes so far as to defend it with passion (or what would pass for passion in such a cold, bleak man), though in other respects he revealed himself, as a general rule, to be a very harsh critic of Rosales. Here, however, he writes a frank apologia for him. The biped without feathers is a *rara avis*, and this queer specimen called Tadeo Requena was all of that and more. Throughout his manuscript, the somewhat insignificant and petty personality of Dr. Rosales possesses Requena, fascinates him, might even be said to obsess him. Despite the palpable loathing that this kind of psychological subjugation arouses in him, despite his impatient efforts to slough it off, he goes back to him again and again, always turning, twisting, and up-braiding him, but never winning control over the situation.

However much he may have wanted to assert himself in the presence of the bedeviled old man, he shows himself ever more insecure in his presence, ever more lacking in self-confidence, ever more suspicious of him. In the beginning, the kindness of his mentor embarrassed him. He asks himself, churlishly, whether that benevolence (condescension is the word he uses) may be nothing more than a way to flatter the Chief. And when the teacher opens wide the treasure chest of his cultural storehouse before the boy's very eyes, he can see no generosity in that display, but only a wish to humiliate him.

The doctor must have felt equally sure that though his neophyte might plunge both hands eagerly into the coffer containing such jewels, he always would come up with a paltry prize compared with what he would have to leave there; and, to cap it all, he would even be compelled to hide this tiny prize as though he had stolen it, for adornments of that kind were in no way suited to him—on him they turned to paste.

I would not go so far as to deny that the young fellow is at least partly right when he thinks that there is a strong streak of vanity in the extemporaneous and erudite boasts of Dr. Rosales. That poor windbag (which is what our little Luisito was, after all) was using the boy as an excuse for giving free rein to his fantastic charlatanry. Yes, Luisito Rosales always had been an eccentric, and his death would later confirm that this eccentricity bordered on the pathological. In that narrow environment of ours, the little fellow kept dreaming of his student days in Paris, a bygone Paris by then, and falsified in memory by imagination to boot. Mired as he was in our raw tropics, he always thought of himself as a *docteur ès lettres* from the Sorbonne, and that is serious. Is it any wonder that the young Tadeo could not understand him? What he kept expecting, and what he would have understood perfectly, was an attitude suitable to one of the gentlemen of San Cosme, to a Rosales, who had taken a boy from that village under his wing owing to a certain set of circumstances, and had gone all out to teach him. And that village boy had adjusted himself to such expectations almost by instinct, almost from the beginning. But to his confusion, nothing turned out that way. At every step the doctor broke the pattern and left him dancing on a slack rope. Tadeo seems to be lost in conjecture, always trying to understand why his teacher is driving himself, working so hard, and taking such great pains with him. The ambiguous phrases of that demented man only confuse him farther; he never is sure whether the man is talking sincerely or making fun of him; he never sees clearly where so much talking and doing are going to end.

Of course all this matter does not pertain either directly or indirectly to the presentation of the historical facts, which the present notes aim to document and clarify as they unfold. Even so, I shall gather together here some of the memoirs of the private secretary, insofar as they have a bearing on his relationship with Dr. Rosales and on his initial contact with the world of gentlemen, which until then he had merely glimpsed. Requena tells us, for example, how he first entered the house in the capital that had been assigned to the Minister of Public Instruction. He is spilling over with satisfaction and a bravado that is a poor cloak for his fear—indeed it tends to proclaim it. The smalltown boy had been longing to meet Don Luisito's children there, but at the same time he was quaking at the mere idea of meeting them face to face; or, to state it more precisely, of meeting María Elena face to face, for he could hardly be bothered over the boy, Angelo.

"María Elena," he tells us later, "greeted me as if she had never seen me before. I was crossing that threshold transformed now into a *brilliant promise. I was a distinguished representative of the new generation which, invigorated by the infusion of blood from the people, constituted the greatest hope of our country.* But that young lady surely thought it generous, discreet, and prudent of her to forget the barefoot tatterdemalion who had been left behind, and to be unable to remember that she had watched him many a time from her balcony or from behind the iron grille as she was taking care of that little dunce of an Angelo, meanwhile amusing herself by staring into the street, while I, like all the others, tried to show off and hand

[38]

her a free ticket to our foolishness, our bragging, that lasted throughout the long, boring village afternoons."

That is what he wrote. He is trying to place himself on top of circumstances in retrospect, and he even muddies the waters knowingly by quoting paragraphs from the newspapers which actually belong to a later time, affecting a tone of irony as he does so. His quotes are from the days when his appointment to the post of secretary to the president had been announced. Consequently, they had nothing to do with the poor guttersnipe whom that madman Luis Rosales introduced to his household on that particular day. He goes on to say that when her father presented him to María Elena as a boy from "our" village of San Cosme, she threw him a "limpid, Olympian" glance (two words that he had doubtless never even heard at the time, another anachronistic item), while Angelo, who had grown into a complete idiot, showed signs of delighted recognition (how could the poor wretched fool dissemble?), thus betraying his sister's impassivity.

A false, studied impassivity that could deceive no one. "So she had never seen me before. Okay! I had a notion to remind her of that time she found a group of us pressed up against the window grille, all quiet as mice, catching flies for Angelo so that we could watch how the loathesome child devoured them. Of course, we ran when we heard her coming, but I can still see the indignation burning in her eyes and scalding her face as she shook that Angelo by the arm. As if it were our fault that he was an idiot. Was she likely to have forgotten that?"

A disgusting scene! And how revealing! Truly, I cannot explain to myself why Luisito had to take that knave into his own home. And I can only answer myself by saying that the man was half out of his mind, so that he should not be blamed for that, or for anything else. He was what is known as an irresponsible, and I am not one of those who think that when he accepted the portfolio offered him by the hangman Bocanegra, he did so because of a sheer talent for vileness. More probably he did it through mere fecklessness, eccentricity, foolishness, or for some reason that no one has thought of. His motives were completely incalculable. If it suddenly occurred to him one day to wax enthusiastic over the young sharper whose education had been turned over to him, he later would think nothing of seating the fellow at his table, after seeing how fast he was progressing and with what ease he was learning. The reaction of the youth himself is typical. If a gentleman like that was treating him that way, it could only be to make fun of him, to cramp his style. The man could only be making a circus of his temporary state of ignorance, his uncouthness, his want of manners; and later (two birds with one stone) he could only be appeasing him against the future when he doubtless would be called to a position in which he could prosper under the resolute and unequivocal patronage of the Chief.

Tadeo finds objectionable, if not reprehensible, everything his preceptor does. Even the teachings from which he was benefiting with such avidity seemed of little practical value to him. "He could not understand," he writes, "that I was not studying to become a scholar of any sort, or that in any case I always would be on the verge of showing my threadbare seams. Ignorant and young though I was, I understood better than he did what suited me and what I needed in order to be able to defend myself in the rough-and-tumble of the world. Fancy touches, useless frills? *A quoi bon, monsieur?*" he asks mockingly. "That veneer which he used to talk about with scorn was precisely what I needed and all that I needed." The style of the memoirs demonstrates, however, that his curiosity, his interest, his application, and his gifts took him far beyond the limits of such a summary apprenticeship. But he had to find something to censure, rightly or wrongly, in anyone who took him up and befriended him.

As I said before, he finds the behavior of Rosales plausible at only one point, and, sure enough, that is the questionable point of his acceptance of the portfolio. To the young Tadeo Requena, the fact that Don Luisito would enter the service of the man who had just assassinated his brother, the senator, far from seeming ignominious, or even cowardly, was a wholly unexpected revelation of his preceptor's intelligence, wisdom, good sense, and discretion. Rosales was demonstrating to him thereby a very keen nose for opportunity, and was proving himself a person prudent enough to be able to pick someone else's brain and clever enough to take whatever profit he could from the situation while looking out for himself at the same time. "The position of minister," he reflects, "is not to be sneered at, and how much less so when it is offered as an alternative to ruin, or even to death. Dr. Rosales," he adds, "was smart enough to realize before it was too late that nowadays no one can oppose the triumph of the people with impunity as his older brother, the odious Don Lucas, had tried to do in all his brutal arrogance. And, after all, what's wrong with accepting reality?" he asks himself.

CHAPTER

6

++++++++++++++++++++++++

Apropos of this man, Don Lucas Rosales: when the item concerning that unnatural violence which, according to rumor, the senator was subjected to in his district is mentioned—also in an incidental way and as a digression—in the memoirs of Secretary Requena, it takes on much greater importance in connection with the present upheavals in our country. A most important source comes to light, one that unquestionably deserves scrupulous prominence, and the details furnished by Tadeo (then loitering in San Cosme, still between childhood and manhood) allow me to establish to my own satisfaction the correct balance of what happened. Few people could boast truthfully of knowing the facts of the barbarous deed perpetrated on the aforementioned senator some time before he was given his quietus with a volley of shots. That "surgical operation" which the Spanish minister did not seem to be entirely convinced was a fact, had indeed been performed, and in what a way! I shall copy verbatim the paragraphs in which Requena gives a detailed account of the deed, for he is not pretending to serve history, though he does. The twist he gives the facts is in accord with the spontaneous bent of his mind; the light in which he shows them is perverted and highly unpleasant to me, but on the other hand, his words possess the unique virtue of authenticity and a direct flavor that I should not like to take away. Insofar as he can, the historian must adduce the original documents that have served him as source material. I am therefore reproducing the very phrases in which Tadeo refers to Senator Lucas Rosales and the cruel outrage that his enemies inflicted on him before they resolved to kill him.

"I can see him now," the private secretary writes; "I can see him big and taciturn, with his wide sombrero pulled down over his forehead, cigar in mouth, and tall leather boots highly polished. No one who remembers his imposing presence would have said that my Don Luisito was a brother of his. To the tenants, his sharecroppers, and the field hands who hated him, that brute used to present the most gigantic expanse of flesh I have ever seen in my life, unless his shadow has grown larger in my memory. He was an awesome sight on horseback; people would lower their heads or turn away their eyes when he went by like a small tornado. But when he was on foot, no man ever failed to take off his hat to him and call him boss and master. So that when he was brought low at last, people hardly dared to believe it. The news brought stupefaction at first, and later, within a few weeks, relief. Even dead and buried he was never mentioned by name except in a low voice."

Requena indulges in some speculations in wretched taste concerning the famous "surgical operation," then goes on to tell what he knows: "I have heard Chino López himself brag about the deed some time after it," he says. "When he was drunk, he sometimes would tell the story of the episode after a lot of coaxing, and would name the place, the day, and the hour. The spot was the dead end road of San José Bendito, which I visited immediately after the event with a gang of other boys. He even named his helpers, all of them outsiders, with details and descriptions that, if they were not sheer invention, at least sounded exaggerated. But the fellow was always far gone in drink; he would talk only when he was in that condition, but he certainly would come out with the whole grisly story then, told with gestures, thumps of his big hands on the table, and guffaws. 'I needed all of five men,' he used to say, 'to strike the blow. I picked some big, strong, willing ones, and it hadn't been easy for me to find them. Hell, no one in San Cosme wanted to take the risk. Everyone hated him; everyone welcomed the idea. But, my friend, when the chips were down the cowards didn't have the guts for it, so we finally had to get hold of some strangers who didn't even know him. Don't you think that was a smart idea? The job got done to perfection, and I'm not bragging when I say so. Every one of those volunteers was given two weeks off and later was promoted to corporal. I've even heard tell that one of them is a non-com in the palace guard now! As for me,' Chino would say mendaciously, 'I didn't want any pay for it, except for the fun I got out of it.' He would go on gabbing and boasting in that vein, but every time he told the story he would vary it in some detail. Still, it is a fact that they did position themselves there in the woods where the path narrows because of the lush growth of the *flamboyante* trees and the bamboo groves. They attacked the landlord by surprise, pulled him off his horse and stuck his head in a bag. Then, as Rosales was held down on the ground, Chino did to the big man what he used to do to the yearling calves and the young bulls. 'You gentlemen may think it's a cinch to do that. But, oh, how the rascal struggled and insulted and threatened.' Chino López would open his mouth wide, his thin moustache would spread across his rotten teeth, and his little eyes would become mere bloodshot slits. 'Oh, work of an angel, my friend!' he boasted. 'I said to him, "Look here, boss, you're going to have to go around cackling like a hen, now. Your rooster days in this barnyard are over." What the hell, I wanted to throw it in his face. Let him recognize me! I didn't care! To tell the whole truth, I wouldn't have felt quite satisfied if His Lordship had never known whose hand had made him an ox. . . .'

[45]

"During the pause that ensued, the Galician, Luna, went up to Chino and asked him, so that everyone could laugh: 'And tell me, Chino, where did you go and hide then, so no one could see your snout for a couple of months?' Indeed, the earth had swallowed up Chino after he had played his nasty prank, and he did not stick his nose out again, and then very cautiously, until he had made sure of the senator's death on the capitol steps. Which is quite logical, after all. No one is going to expose himself to the vengeance of the powerful. Whatever the promises made to them, the lowborn never can keep their backs entirely covered, make no mistake about that. And even though the deceased had left only two young sons, still minors, he did have friends and this brother, the doctor, who was an unknown at the time, for until then he had never held any position of responsibility or prestige. The widow, who also was in danger, emigrated with her children. Don Luisito came down on the side of reason—the dead cannot be resurrected—and the passing of time did the rest."

That is all he has to say about it. The young, jumped-up secretary ends this story of his, as always, with the colophon of his dubious moralizations. Of course he does not say that he had been enjoying himself, but his gloating pervades everything as he fingers the details of the repulsive scene of Chino airing his exploits in the saloon. I ask myself what Sir Private Secretary Tadeo Requena would have thought if he had known the end the fates were holding in store for Chino López, what they were delightedly promising themselves: that he would be hanged head down and forced to swallow his own private parts.

CHAPTER

7

++++++++++++++++++++++++++

But no. In all likelihood he would not have
been in the least astonished. Of course he would not have been.
Nothing could frighten Tadeo; nothing, good or bad, lucky or
unlucky, seemed to surprise him. He was an imperturbable creature; nothing could move him, and anyone might believe that
what kept him on an even keel, at least outwardly, was the
virtue of stoicism, were it not that a hair of the shrewd yokel
would peep out sometimes beneath that covering of apathy.
That Tadeo Requena! The fellow is no longer living now; what
a pity not to have paid more attention to him, not to have observed him more closely while he was still alive! But, who could
have guessed . . . ?

Although he never opened his mouth, we have him right here
before us as we study his memoirs with care. He tells the continued story of his liberally bestowed career, step by step. He
accepts an appointment and collects a salary as a temporary

official of secondary rank with the greatest naturalness—so as to defray the expenses of his studies, he explains. Yet he had no duties beyond going to sign his name at the end of each month. Straightaway—yes, immediately—he is granted a degree of Doctor of Laws and Social Sciences, only God and Luisito Rosales know how, in order to take over the position of private secretary to His Excellency without wasting any time and to be installed in the National Palace, where the Chief would have him instantly on call at all times. All those things are mere whims of fortune to him. He accepts her free gifts without blinking an eye. Perhaps he thinks he does not deserve all that. Perhaps he thinks in his heart that no one deserves anything; let anyone who wins the lottery enjoy it in peace.

Once he is installed as secretary, his sullenness, his paucity of words, and an austere frown serve him as battlements. He never leaves exposed the flanks of his educational deficiencies, his ill-mended ignorance. He wraps himself in a wary silence and issues peremptory orders, passes on instructions, avoids making decisions. Meanwhile, he is observing, listening, taking note of everything that happens, and above all, he is writing, writing, writing. In the secrecy of his memoirs, he phrases his commentaries (seldom openly expressed, more frequently implicit), which he never would have dared give voice to.

Beneath his cloak of inveterate cold-bloodedness, we can see him as he describes with perceptible satisfaction, but at the same time with a critical eye, the incidents of the celebration of the national holiday during which he first appeared in His Excellency's suite. It amuses him to give in exact detail the order in which the retinue was lined up, the variety of the uniforms, the several acts, the ceremonies, the appearance of the crowd. It affords him boundless satisfaction to see himself inside the presidential box on the platform during the parade, although he would like to conceal it even from himself. That moment brought back to mind the jest uttered by the Galician, Luna, who once had prophesied—he phrases it as a prophecy —in alluding to his physical resemblance to Bocanegra, that the troops would salute him as they marched by. "Of course," he reflects, "on this present occasion the salute was not directed at me in particular as yet, but rather to everyone there on the flag-draped platform, decorated with banners and coats of arms, and first of all to the Chief, who was standing motionless as a statute in the center of the first row between the archbishop and the Minister of War, poor General Malagarriga, who was all unaware that this would be his last patriotic celebration. All the other government ministers were lined up behind them, and, farther back, no longer with any regard for preferential rank, the other high officials of the presidential mansion, among whom I held a very conspicuous place. The grenadiers of the guard, lined up in perfect formation, were covering and shielding the speaker's stand.

"What with one thing and another, the parade had got off to a late start near noon," the young Tadeo goes on, "and though it was early in the year for extreme heat, being only the 28th of February (the national holiday actually falls on the 29th, and it is general knowledge that our glorious Freedom Cry was uttered on a Saturday, the 29th of February, although we are not going to wait for the leap years to celebrate it), nonetheless the sun was beating down mercilessly, filtering through a mass of clouds that seemed on the verge of discharging their burden. Even before the parade started, ambulances had had to take away three or four soldiers from the lines; and there on the platform I was amusing myself by watching how General Malagarriga, half-suffocated and on the verge of a sunstroke, kept running his finger around the inside of the collar of his uniform to pull it away from his flesh, trying to draw in his neck like a turtle, or else using his handkerchief to mop up the sweat streaming down from the band of his cap. The prelate was also sweating rivers, and of them all, only our Chief, Bocanegra, seemed immune to any fatigue, invulnerable to the scourge of the sun, and delighted with the spectacle, absorbed in it, if not downright pleased to be putting the weakness of his colleagues to the test, for he was an admirer of a Spartan training.

"How the celebration lagged, and dragged, and dragged interminably! The parade was lasting for hours, and even to one who was witnessing such a brilliant review for the first time, its length finally became a nightmare. I don't know how many times since morning our two air squadrons had performed their maneuvers in the blue. We had watched our best troops of the line pass endlessly before the platform, plus the artillery, the cavalry, the motorized units, the auxiliary services, always with a big gap between one unit and the next, one corps and the next. But at long last it seemed that the parade was about to come to a close with what was to be the star turn and the novelty of that year—the mighty brigade of the reconstituted mounted police, under the command of Pancho Cortina. They had kept in close formation in front of our platform, under such strict discipline—all the horses perfectly in line, all the men stiff and erect, their weapons and patent leather hats glistening—that they offered an almost pitiful contrast to the ragged march and unmatched equipment of the regular army. After all, what matters most here is the number of the troops, even if at the expense of quality, which never could amount to much either, given our human source material. The success of the debut of our new mounted police was so flattering that on the following day Pancho Cortina, their new commandant, was rewarded with a promotion by decree in the Official Gazette. As a matter of fact—and this is a secret known to few people—the guarding of His Excellency during the performance was the responsibility of that brilliant police force stationed there in front of the platform as being more trustworthy than the decorative presidential bodyguard, positioned just beneath the stand.

"Now, at that very moment, the evolution of the police was getting under way. Pancho was making his horse curvet, and, with his saber aloft in salute, was offering the president his movie-star smile and was taking his place, while the regimental band of the lancers from Tucaití was launching into the strains of the national anthem. At that moment I glanced at the Chief. Firmly planted, standing stiffly, his eyes half-closed, he was listening to the music, the symbol of our national hope and glory, while the crowd of soldiers and civilians filling the great wide esplanade—troops and the public—were holding the composed, solemn attitude that is proper when the national anthem is about to be sung.

"I don't know whether I was overtired by then, but the fact is that, after a time this, too, seemed to drag beyond all reckoning. The music went on and on endlessly. People began to stare at one another, yet Bocanegra did not put a stop to it by giving the bandleader the usual signal to bring to a close the performance of that venerable piece. Among the other peculiarities of our national anthem, it happens to lack any proper beginning or end. It consists of only one theme, as simple, short, and grandiose as our history, a motif that is developed, varied, and repeated in two distinct rhythms, one very slow and the other very fast, and the alternate use of them results in a noble and dramatic contrast. Those who criticize it can't see that. Perhaps it is a vulgar little tune—I don't know a thing about music—but it ought to move every good citizen. At least it has the merit of being the work of one of our own composers; we did not have to turn to foreign inspiration like our arrogant neighbors who, for all their pretension to great power, can never deny that they owe their national anthem to the good offices of a Catalan artist. Be ours as modest as you like, it is at least the fruit of native talent, and its words, conceived within the framework of the great Hispano-American traditions, echo those concepts which used to mortify the businessmen from Spain who were poorly reconciled to the idea that our tiny republic—a new David—had succeeded in conquering the Mother Country and in breaking her chains, thus humbling the haughty lion that serves as her symbol.

"The public had been singing in chorus at first, but later the voices dwindled, fell off, while the band, on the other hand, went on playing, undaunted, repeating the fast rhythms after pouring out the preceding slow ones, drop by drop, only to go back to them in turn. Of course, each section is usually repeated only three times, which is quite enough. Generally only the words of the first three stanzas are sung. But in the course of public functions, in the presence of the president and out of

[51]

respect for him, the music goes on until His Excellency indicates by a slight nod of his head that he considers himself satisfied. The bandleader was watching anxiously for that signal —anxiously, but in vain, for Bocanegra seemed lost in the clouds. We members of his retinue were watching him uneasily, too, but he never made a move. The scene was beginning to take on the aspect of a remote and disturbing dream; we were sweltering in the sun, the parade seemed to glitter insubstantially in the hazy air, and the music dragged on as if it would trickle away at any moment. And then, lo and behold, a dog suddenly began to bark furiously at the hooves of the bodyguard's horses. It would be impossible to convey even a notion of the very strange effect produced by that unexpected and incongruous note in the midst of such solemnity. No doubt it was a small dog, but it was barking with such stridency and sustained rage that the noise seemed to get entangled in the harmonies of the band, and at times, even to dominate the melody. It was something really ridiculous, funny, undignified, I don't know what.

"And yet with it all, Bocanegra remained in the same pose, seemingly absent-minded, with no intention of taking any notice of anything. The miserable fellow often enjoys doing things like that; he might almost be said to have a touch of madness. But that was not the end of it. As if that were not enough, and perhaps because nonsense begets nonsense, I suddenly noticed that Dr. Rosales was beginning to move along his row, that he was leaving his government colleagues. And in the middle of this incredible situation he began with a very resolute air to go down the steps from the platform. I became apprehensive. Where could he be going? Then, believe it or not, that big fool went up to the dog, without commending himself to God or the Devil, and delivered it a fierce kick in front of the numberless eyes of the troops and the public. From where I was sitting I did not realize what was happening until I heard the angry barking suddenly change to pitiful howls and saw the little dog cross the street on the run and finally lose himself among the legs of the crowd just as the doctor, very pompous, went back to his place on the platform.

"Finally, then, the president gave his long-awaited little nod, and the music was extinguished after one more repetition of the final measures, which kept echoing on and on, obsessively, like a refrain running from the lips to the depths of every heart: *'Conquered, yes conquered, the haughty lion'*."

CHAPTER

8

✦✦✦✦✦✦✦✦✦✦✦✦✦✦✦✦✦✦✦✦✦✦✦✦✦

I wanted to laugh when I came across the reference in Tadeo's memoirs to that absurd story of the impudent little dog and the zealous minister. Over the years, I had forgotten completely that episode, which had been so much talked of in its day. And the truth is that in the midst of the present unrest, in this atmosphere supercharged with serious threats, the storm of petty argument that such a trivial and laughable incident could unleash in those days seems absurd in recollection. To be sure, we had too few subjects to occupy our minds at that time, and any bit of nonsense was turned over a hundred times, until it assumed colossal proportions. Besides, in this case it occurred through an act of the eccentric Luisito Rosales, whom many people detested because he had surrendered—sold out, they used to say—and entered the service of the dictator. Those implacable critics could see the full scope of an abject adulation of Bocanegra in the silly action taken by Don Luisito, the very depths of indignity, instead of an obvious symptom of his mental state. Others, more reasonable, did not condemn the poor wretch, but condemned instead a regime capable of keeping such a buffoon at the head of the system of public education.

As far as I can recall, only Camarasa took it upon himself— largely to be contrary—to defend the minister who had stepped down from his place on the platform to deliver a kick to the disturbing little animal. "What Rosales did," Camarasa maintained, in his usual irritating manner, "contains a practical lesson in democracy for any bemedaled personage, and he was therefore well within his function as Minister of Public Instruction." He went on to ask, "Would anyone like to bet that if Bocanegra himself had done a thing like that, everyone would be singing his praises and his wonders right now?" As was always the case with Camarasa, no one knew for sure whether he was talking nonsense in all seriousness or whether he was pulling legs. The fact is that it took a lot of patience to put up with his constant kidding tone.

As for Secretary Requena, it could not have been easy for him either—as we go back to his memoirs—to be absolutely sure of his own reaction to the idiocy of Rosales. His attitude wears the air of a kind of strange expectancy, not untouched with anxiety, an ambivalent suspension of judgment, which corresponds to and is mated with the succession of his feelings toward Rosales revealed from the beginning. For example, the relief he admits at finding Don Luisito the first time he was brought into Bocanegra's presence will be recalled, and that that relief vanished instantly before the thought that the man would have no notion whatever of who he was. Again he doubts and is surprised to learn that Rosales not only showed plainly that he recognized him, but even gave him a friendly slap on the back and inquired about his mother, "that good woman, Doña Belén," at the moment when Bocanegra turned over to him the education of "this young fellow-townsman of yours." But in the end, he is never able to rid himself of suspicion, and he figures that the kindhearted arrangements of his preceptor could mean nothing but obsequiousness to the Chief, that the pedagogue's conscientiousness was born of his fondness for talking and for showing off how much he knew, and that he was using his pupil as an excuse for giving rein to his inexhaustible loquacity.

"Surely," Requena reflects in a certain passage, "such an outstanding patrician would have been delighted to indoctrinate and cram with learning, not some hapless nobody like me, but his only son and the heir to his glory. But as is often the way of the world, his scion was a congenital idiot; alas, he could count on Angelo for nothing. The kid used to while away the hours drooling in the window, and it was a great treat for the poor cretin when some village boy, some ragged, hungry urchin, like this Tadeo—to go no further—would go up to him with the mischievous intention of playing some scurvy trick on him. Yes, he is the one Don Luisito would have loved to teach his arts and sciences. Tough luck, my friend!"

Tadeo ends his account of the celebration of the first national holiday he had ever attended as private secretary to His Excellency with a reference to the military parade and the succeeding commentaries and news: "It is a strange thing that out of all that happened during the ceremony," he writes, "the nonsense over the dog keeps running through my mind, and it has brought on an unreasonable sense of uneasiness; unreasonable, I say, for, after all, discordant notes, picturesque details, funny little happenings, impromptu interludes never are lacking in the splendor of a day like that, and may even heighten the solemnity of the occasion. But, as far as I can see, I was not the only one whom Dr. Rosales had shocked by his blunder, for when I went back to my office at the end of the ceremony, I quickly realize that the conversation of the personnel on the other side of the screen was revolving around that very theme. They had not heard me come in, and Sobrarbe, unaware that he was being overheard, was commenting jokingly on the episode, to the delight of the two ladies who, with him, constitute the secretarial staff under my orders. The news already had flown far. Despite the festiveness of the day, they were on duty, ready for any contingency, and Sobrarbe, that busybody, had been playing hooky from his duties and had scurried off to watch the parade. Now he was clowning, with his affected z's and s's and his annoying little titters, making fun of the minister in front of his fellow workers. I cannot stand Sobrarbe, and Adelita annoys me with her excessively servile attitude, while Doña Angustias is going through all the ups and downs of an already overlong menopause and forcing everyone to go through them with her. But I put up with my three trained seals because at least they are familiar with the administrative routine and what we might call the customs of the household. It was a blessing for me to find that small staff there, so highly skilled that I only had to give an order—or, in most cases, to transmit one, especially at the time I was put in charge of the secretary's office—to have them carry it out without forgetting any of the details and requirements and fuss, which I never would have been able to keep in mind. I am continuing the same practice to this day, and things seem to do themselves, so to speak. Bocanegra tells me what he wants and I put the machinery into motion; then the Chief's instructions are carried out in no time. And it has happened more than once that even the ministers are alerted to the decrees having to do with their respective departments through reading about them in the Official Gazette or even through news in the daily press.

"That is precisely what was to happen with regard to the promotion of Pancho Cortina that day. After our return from the celebration, as we were climbing the main stairway to the palace, the president takes me by the arm and asks me: 'How did it go? What did you think of the parade? Impressive, wasn't it? Especially that last touch with the mounted police. That Pancho has really outdone himself, and he ought to be rewarded for it; he's earned a promotion. We're going to make him a colonel, Tadeo. You bring me the decree to sign so we can give the kid a big surprise tomorrow.'

"Be it said parenthetically that the man who was to get the big surprise was the Minister of War, General Malagarriga, who called me on the telephone the next day and rebuked me, call-

ing me 'boy', with the greatest acrimony. 'Listen here, boy . . .'
I explained the circumstance as it had occurred; that those were
His Excellency's orders, so . . . 'There's no excuse, boy,' he
shouted from the other end of the wire, like a man possessed;
'If the president decides to put the suggestion I had just made
him verbally into immediate effect . . .'—I was laughing up
my sleeve as I listened to him; I was indeed—'. . . that does
not excuse you, boy, for not going through the proper channels. Couldn't you perhaps have sent me the text of the order
for my okay by the same motorcycle messenger who took it to
the press?' He would not be placated; it seems they had called
him from the editorial office of *El Comercio* asking him to confirm the news of the promotion and comment on it, and he had
been so astounded that he did not know what to say. Besides,
he was right. I recognize that. It would have been better to
have done as he said. When on the following morning they
brought him the document so that *a posteriori* he could sign it,
it was already too late to correct the oversight. The man was as
good as finished, and the decree would go into the files without
the minister's signature. But a man cannot foresee everything
or be up on everything. When Bocanegra took it into his head
to do something on the spur of the moment, everyone had to
walk softly!

"That day, in spite of the weariness I felt after the famous
parade and all those hours of standing on the platform, I had
no sooner been given the order than I sent the doorman out
to bring a sandwich and a beer to me in my office and, while
I was listening to the personnel amusing themselves over the
kick the doctor had given the noisy little dog, I was roughing
out some phrases, correcting them, and at the same time ringing
my buzzer. 'See here, Adelita, you people are to draw up a
decree by the Minister of War promoting (note that) Lieutenant
Colonel Don Francisco Cortina, the reorganizer of the Services
for the General Direction of the Security of the State and Commandant of the Mounted Police, to the rank immediately above
—that is, to colonel—retaining the same job and command. Do
it like lightning, do you understand? The reasons for the decree

(make a note of this, Adelita) are the following (write them down): extraordinary zeal in the execution of the commissions entrusted to him, and a praiseworthy capacity for organization demonstrated as the head of the Special Corps of Mounted Police, *et cetera.*'

"No sooner had I finished my cold and scanty lunch than the text of the decree was ready for signature, with the proper seal and all the rest. Bocanegra signed it almost without bothering to read it (such was the confidence he had in me), pushing his plate a little to one side, for when I brought it to him, they were all still at the table. The *señora,* seated in her place invited me: 'Sit down and eat with us, Requena.' But before I could answer her that I had already had had lunch, thank you very much, Bocanegra answered for me. 'This young man has to rush off right now. When everything is ready,' he added, addressing me, 'and you have made sure that it has gone to press, come and have coffee with us.' Even invitations take the form of commands on the lips of Bocanegra," the secretary comments.

I ask myself whether this observation of Tadeo's is meant as a criticism, whether it expresses resentment, or whether it oozes admiration. I am not sure what the answer is, though I am inclined to think that all three emotions may have mingled in his mind, without his being entirely aware of them. In general, the young Tadeo appears to understand Antón Bocanegra, that former Father of the Poor, very well. The opposite occurred with Dr. Rosales, who always upset Requena, always made him feel uncomfortable, and who was a living enigma to him when all is said and done. Whether or not Requena accepted the president and approved of him is another question. Whether he actually admired him, feared him, respected him, even perhaps hated him at times, is very difficult to determine, but in any case it is evident that he understood him perfectly. He speaks of him as if he were speaking of the weather, as a fact which it would not even have occurred to him to question. "Even invitations take the form of commands on Bocanegra's lips." That is the way it is, and that's enough, isn't it?

All of that seems the most natural thing in the world to

Tadeo Requena. He does not even remark on his master's brutal lack of consideration. We already have witnessed with what indifference, with what repulsive coldness, he refers to the harm done to my uncle, poor Antenor Malagarriga, an injury that undoubtedly cost him his life. My uncle was a weak man, to be sure, and he had done wrong, of course, in assuming the war portfolio—at long last, from his point of view—but with all his faults, he was not a rascal like the rest, but on the contrary, a perfect gentleman and a most dutiful soldier. The lack of respect with which that shameless scoundrel reports his death! To him, the only thing to be regretted was that the general could not put his own signature on the decree, which therefore had to be filed without that requisite. . . Each time I read those paragraphs, indignation boils up in my chest again, not because it had to do with a relative of mine, and a good man, but because it reveals what kind of trash has us in its grip. Not without cause has our country rolled to the edge of the abyss, where it is struggling right now, weeping, and bleeding.

CHAPTER

9

✦✦✦✦✦✦✦✦✦✦✦✦✦✦✦✦✦✦✦✦✦✦✦✦✦

They all understood one another very well,
though they also would destroy one another in the end. Yes,
the faithful private secretary, the watchdog, would wind up by
assassinating his master, but what difference did it make? That
could not alter the fact that from the first moment, his relations with his boss had been easy and as smooth as silk. With
peasant shrewdness, Tadeo had assumed the most passive of
attitudes, keeping his mouth shut, lying low, obeying, making
himself small, and eschewing any initiative, with the result that
his chief, The Chief, began to make use of him little by little,
and to try him out as he needed him, so as to make him quickly
into his intimate and indispensable tool. That was surely what
he had been planning for some time, what he wanted and loved,
without ever dreaming that this tool of his would turn against
him and become the instrument of his death. Certainly they were
two of a kind. With what crude satisfaction the secretary ap-

plauds Bocanegra's insolence, and how he gloats over the nasty triumphs that his master achieves by means of others' weaknesses, miserable qualities, and vilenesses!

To be sure, the degradation of our public environment could hardly fail to offer abundant material for frequent spectacles of abjectness. Here it might be appropriate to interpolate the story of one of them, as extracted from Requena's manuscript. This oaf (let him deceive those who do not know him as I know him now, with his pretensions to being a clandestine writer!) describes President Bocanegra's induction into the National Academy of Arts and Letters, a function that I also had occasion to attend, and therefore was able to witness from the platform for special guests. He permits himself to wax sarcastic as he describes that orgy of bestiality and humiliation, which left me indignant, depressed, and filled with loathing, as I remember vividly.

Insolently, Tadeo indulges in irony: "The ceremony was good, very good. And Dr. Rosales, who had sweated to try to achieve his greatest success, can sleep the sleep of a gratified man tonight. Tomorrow morning the newspapers will praise the function as very brilliant, and justly. Our illustrious president, already an honorary doctor, now has been awarded the academic palm. If he wanted to, he could display in turn, or in combination, his doctor's mortarboard, the academician's dress sword, the marshal's baton, the shoulder-boards of an admiral, even—and why not?—the cardinal's hat, following in the footsteps of many other heads of state. But no, indeed, our Bocanegra does not reward himself with trinkets. Instead of displaying those decorations, he likes to show off only one symbol of his power —the silver spurs, which never have ceased to jingle at his heels, though he never has let himself be seen on horseback.

"Well, then, the man arrived with his boots and his spurs and his shirt unbuttoned down the front, to seat himself among the parrots from the academy, next to his dignified Minister of Public Instruction (who had tried in vain to suggest to him in every kind of roundabout way the propriety of wearing at least a dinner jacket, if not a tailcoat) and to the right of the president of the learned body, our decrepit poet laureate, Don Hermenegildo del Olmo, who, though obsequious and stupid, looked very decorative with his shock of white hair above the green velvet hood embroidered with scrolls and sprinkled with dandruff. Between them, with his legs sprawled out, Bocanegra spent the entire time of the speeches, which was not short, staring at the ceiling with his arms crossed and a vacant expression on his face. But in the meantime, the performance flowed on very brilliantly, as I say. Naturally, no one was absent. The caparisoned luminaries, slated for immortality, all occupied their chairs, plus the candidates who were to achieve it sooner or later—the journalists, professors of art or Spanish literature, week-end poets—and who were grouped together on the platform, eager to be seen.

"Not illogically, the Chief looks at all those begowned people, but does not see them. I myself, who they would doubtless consider a perfect nullity, completely alien to the graces of good speech, which they cultivate, nevertheless am an object of the most polished deference whenever I am within hand's reach of them, for no other reason than that I am private secretary to the All-Powerful and because they know that the minister considers me his pupil. When a man was once nothing but a stray cat in a ditch beside the road, a pariah, an ignoramus, he may very well feel some respect for those who can write prettily, have their verses published in the newspapers, and speak over the radio. Why should I deny my erstwhile enthusiasm for the great figures of our Parnassus, and particularly for Carmelo Zapata? Although he is—or perhaps precisely because he is—a Negro, he is recognized and proclaimed *urbe et orbi* as our leading young poet, from whom no one has ever dreamed of snatching that honorable title, even though his fame has been on the wane for forty years. Every Sunday he used to regale us *in secula seculorum* in the distinguished book section of *El Comercio* with his matchless lyrical outpourings, often worthy of the pen of Rubén Darío himself, no matter how loudly his detractors might laugh at the fact that Rodríguez, the Galician, had to correct the spelling and the versification here and there while

[65]

editing them. Why didn't the Galician write the verses himself if he was so able? After all, spelling and the rules of composition are mechanical skills that anyone can learn, and no one but pedants like Rodríguez would make an issue of that—no one but the Pharisees of culture.

"Later, with the passing of time, I came to know them all —the Negro Zapata, and those not like him. Why talk about it? Every time I run afoul of one of those luminaries, I purposely set out to exaggerate the crudeness of my manners and my speech. Don't they take me for a literate barbarian? Then let them leave me to the enjoyment of the spectacle of their flattery whenever they come to wheedle me into doing some little administrative favor for them. Those wretches never would suspect that this ignoramus, this sandbank doctor, callow, uncultivated as I know they call me, could, if he wanted to, display literary abilities superior to theirs. I feel sure that before long they themselves will clamor to come and offer me the honor of their guild, and will be pleased as Punch to be able to admit to their inner sanctum the young and distinguished private secretary to His Excellency. And I see no reason why the seat of my pants would be such a bad fit there as long as Zapata occupies a plush seat wherein to deposit his voluminous backside.

"But no, I must not harbor such a thought. On the one hand, the mere idea of participating in that vanity fair makes me feel ashamed. On the other hand I don't like to watch a spectacle like today's from the dress circle, or even from the guest platform, as I did this time. I'd rather watch from the shadows of some obscure corner where I can see everything without being seen. There I am free to amuse myself by watching the Chief sprawled out in a chair in his jackboots and with his shirt unbuttoned down the front in the midst of the illustrious body met in his honor. And you may be sure I would have given a good deal to be able to enter Bocanegra's mind as he drowsed there like a crocodile in the sun, the while the sociologist Toño Zaralegui, to name only one, was holding forth categorically on the peculiarities of our national idiom, that expression of the genius of the fatherland, so greatly enriched by the contribution made through the proclamations, speeches, and decrees of that extraordinary man, Antón Bocanegra, one of the appointed number of our academicians, in whose unmistakable and vigorous style, fruit of an original mind, pulses the might of a new race already slated for the most brilliant destiny, *et cetera, et cetera, et cetera*. The president's face was reflecting nothing. And as for Dr. Rosales, who was His Excellency's ghost writer, as I knew very well, he did not betray any awareness of the effect the dithyrambs his colleague was pouring forth at such length was having upon him. I was watching, with malice aforethought, trying to glimpse in his expression some trace of a swollen head, of vainglory, of fear, of something; but my little man was hanging so tightly onto the organization of the affair, walking on red hot coals, so terrified of some slip, that it all went over his head, and he did not even stop to think that the only literary values invoked by initiating the new member into the academy were the work of his own learned pen."

CHAPTER

10

+++++++++++++++++++++++++++++

I shall not go on copying; that is enough. Enough
of so much suppressed pride, of so much thwarted ability, of so
much concealed arrogance; but above all enough—because no
one could put up with any more—of that mordacity which, like
an acid, destroys whatever it touches. How awful—and how unexpected—this Tadeo Requena turns out to be in his memoirs!
In view of these times of unscrupulous aggressors, times when,
with all the dams broken, nothing appears impossible or excessive to anyone, it could hardly be more than a minor surprise
to find in him a sapling with absurd pretensions. Who would not
have taken the young secretary for a very conspicuous climber, always on the lookout for the main chance, capable of daring anything, though more ignorant and less gifted than he actually
was? Who would have ventured to prophesy what he would
eventually come to: crime, and finally a headlong fall, for on
that battleground where the high command is surrounded by in-

trigues and snares, a fellow like that would hardly be rated higher than a poor simpleton without any subtlety, without malleability, without any talent beyond mad audacity. A wretched yokel! His real talent and his strength were of another kind— quite formidable, even demoniac. It lay in the corrosive power of a look that could vaporize, dissipate, empty, corrupt—in short, destroy—any object that it lighted upon, leaving it stripped down to its ridiculous nakedness. A tremendous power, which he himself may not have been aware of, or not fully aware of, as if by a sort of X ray he could see the skull beneath the scalp and an absurd dance of skeletons in everyone's movements; a power that he exercised without planning to, without wanting to. Who knows but that he turned it against himself, and that it was the fundamental cause of his ultimate ruin, for at what point and in what way can the chain of disintegration be broken?

That is the great surprise wrapped up in the memoirs: the loathsome lucidity—loathsome and fascinating, for I must confess that it fascinates me at times—of such a glance. That cruel camera, that implacable objectivity, detached and hidden, for years was registering everything taking place in the "upper spheres," and no one ever suspected it. Tadeo Requena gives a glimpse into the interior of the home of the tyrant and of the woman whom the newspapers always called the First Lady of the Republic. He introduces us into those evening conversational gatherings at which she used to reign, joking and laughing, unconsciously, or perhaps not so unconsciously, playing the role of *agent provocateur,* in part at least, while Bocanegra sat silent and watching, watching and sitting silent, until he made the guests, too deeply involved with their talking and drinking, forget that he was laying an ambush for them. Actually those intimate gatherings were rightly hers, and he did no more than show his snout there from time to time as a condescending guest, taking little part in the conversation of those who were paying court to his wife. Tadeo also reveals to us through his memoirs the boredom of other nights when they sat there alone as, yawning and grunting, the ruling couple sat face to face at last, while he, Tadeo Requena, a person so much a part of the family that he finally ceased to exist for them, wanders to and fro, and vanishes finally without saying good night.

"He, dozing and brutish," Tadeo says in a paragraph that would provide food for thought for those who know the ending of this story, "with a glass of rum always within hand's reach; she, her eyes puffy, inattentive, schemes, weaves plots, and tirelessly spins malevolent intrigues. Who is holding up the edifice of public order now? Who is guarding the sanctum of the power? The servants have withdrawn some time ago. There is no one in the offices; the telegrapher on shift is dozing, too, head on arms, or is reading a novel without an end. Even the captain of the guard will be taking a short nap down below, leaving it to others to cope with his boring routine. And finally I vanish. Outdoors, the city and the country, lie sunk in slumber. Everything roundabout is in darkness, everything in silence, and in the anteroom nothing can be heard but an occasional creak and the ticking of the clock, gnawing away time. Night has come and, as if suddenly, the implacable struggle has died down for a few hours. No one is waiting outside this room to approach this desk, which is a ramport of contentiousness, a dike against pressures, against impatience, against great and small ambitions; against the brute force of the impetuous, the clever traps of the sly, the solicitations, the vain deceits, cajolery, intrigue, bribery, the artful scheme, the maneuver planned in hollow-eyed wakefulness and premeditation, the daring stroke, all the more frightening for having failed visibly. A truce has been declared, and everyone is asleep. Sometimes I like to wander at that time of night through the vacant parlors or to stare out for a while from a balcony at the empty parade ground." Even his reports concerning official receptions, despite the full descriptions of these events given to the public by the morning papers, can be of interest. For he includes some unpublished material containing special meaning and his uncanny linking of evidence shows up some illuminating detail.

The data the secretary offers us almost always embrace some curious fact, which may or may not in itself turn out to be transcendental or even important. At times the importance may lie in a relation to events subsequent to that moment, or may be consequent to something with an importance not yet foreseen, but which becomes clear in retrospect. An instance of that is what Tadeo has to say about Bocanegra's habits as a drinking man. He himself was far from guessing, at the time he mentioned them, how great their personal and historical scope would be, how those habits of the president would play a part in Bocanegra's tragedy. Requena notes them probably for the sheer pleasure of slandering him. Be that as it may, many people were unaware of Bocanegra's predilection, indeed his exclusive fondness for the rum made from the native sugar cane, and Requena clears up that point for us.

"The greatest proof of the confidence he has placed in me, I think, is that he entrusts me with the task of filling his glass," Secretary Requena writes, and then adds: "He drinks only rum; he doesn't like anything else. At the official functions, the great receptions, and even at less solemn gatherings, champagne is drunk, cocktails are served, and the mainstay is always scotch whisky. But when it comes to drinking, our president reveals a fanatical patriotism and will not compromise. No one could take his rum away from him. Of course, it was poured from fine crystal decanters (for the forms must be observed) identical with the whisky decanters, so that from the outside no one could notice any difference. In this way, he neither forces his tastes on anyone nor has to expose himself to the criticism of the gilded crowd with its fine, expensive, exquisite, and snobbish drinks. Every time the newspapers present photographic testimony to the chats held by His Excellency at the doors of the cabins, in the open fields, or in front of the low-class saloons in the suburbs where he likes to stop from time to time to mingle with the unwashed, and where, of course, he accepts his unfailing tipple, he doubtless is admired for such a sacrifice on the altar of popular taste. I can certify, however, that none of that involves a sacrifice. That very liquor is what mitigates his infrequent evenings with his family, that is what he orders served to him on the sly at the most elegant soirées, and it falls to me, unfailingly, to be the guardian and *sommelier* of his secret. My duty consists in handing him one glass after another, with no pauses between. How many times have I watched him begin to stare fixedly after a while, how often have I seen his features turn wooden and his mind become dulled into a kind of taciturn stubbornness, while all around him everyone was growing livelier, laughter was becoming contagious, people were turning silly? How many times have I attributed that difference less to the sinister character, which so many who do not know him well impute to our Chief—I say, how often has it occurred to me to attribute those results to the full-bodied, popular pain-killer rather than to his temperament. Bocanegra maintains contact with his beloved common people by drinking rum in a cut-glass disguise; he remains faithful to the sordid hard drinking of the populace while all those ex-sergeants, ex-newspapermen, ex-nobodies, now magistrates, general directors, bankers, and ministers, together with the foreign diplomats often of analogous extraction, are in their glory, gay, happy, mingling with the elated wives, whose arms or rumps they caress on the sly whenever the opportunity is at hand. If they were not in such a state, they would doubtless tremble at the sight of the tigerish glare that rum confers on the Chief. But they notice nothing whatever, decked out in their fine clothes, euphoric, loquacious, fat, smiling. I notice everything, for I don't drink—I, who keep filling the goblet.

'Ah, if only people knew how to observe, how many surprises they would be spared, how many of them would be able in time to parry the blow or dodge it! I am astonished that the president has placed such blind confidence in me, for he knows that I remain sober beside him while he drinks and drinks, and that in certain cases it is enough for me to follow the direction of his eyes to guess his intentions. This happened not long ago with Domenech, shot in one leap from the lazy man's job of manager of the National Bank for Credit and Subsidies to the dungeons beneath the palace. What to everyone else was a thunderbolt and the father and mother of sensations was no surprise to me. Why? Well, because three days earlier, at the reception and dance for the Mexican ambassador, as I was waiting for the Chief to drain the last sip from his glass before instantly serving him another, I grasped the fact that the fate of Domenech was sealed merely by noticing the long, cold, steady, unwinking stare that the Chief had fixed

on him as he was babbling some endless phrase or other, without
a care in the world as he entertained and delighted the lickspittles
who always surrounded him. Quite oblivious of everything,
Domenech had sequestered himself in a corner of the drawing
room with the United States commercial attaché. So engulfed was
the gentleman in his own subject that he did not even sense
Bocanegra's oppressive stare fastened upon him. Bocanegra, on
the other hand, in spite of all the rum he had in him, was very
well aware that I was following the course of his thought along
the dotted line of his stare. And on a later day he did not forget
it. When I went to him early in the morning to have him sign
some documents, he said, without looking at me, as he was busily
stirring his coffee with his spoon, 'That Domenech is a highway
robber, did you know that?' Then he added, 'You're bound to see
a good deal because you're young and you're nobody's fool.' Perhaps for that very reason, because he did not consider me a fool,
because he wanted me to learn, and because he knew I was learning after all, he gave me the job, along with Pancho Cortina, of
arresting Domenech and holding him incommunicado, while the
Secretary of the Treasury ordered all his accounts, his money, his
other goods movable and immovable, attached, without sparing
even his personal effects. Domenech was a thief, that was hot
news! Besides, was he the only thief, even the most notorious one?
What cause, reason or motive His Excellency had for suddenly
taking notice of it is something I don't know yet."

CHAPTER

11

++++++++++++++++++++++++++++++

"In any case, and with reference to what has to do with me," Tadeo goes on, "it seems clear that the president is making me more and more a trusted intimate, and that he is planning to use me for some scheme of his, for some circumstance or other that is worth a special amount of pains to him. Such things need not necessarily be risky or even what the pusillanimous might consider unpleasant. As in the classical theater, a comic interlude is interpolated from time to time into the middle of most performances of tragedies.

"The episode, which we might entitle The Kidnapped Child, belongs to this genre. It fell to me to take a part in the unravelling of the plot, at the special behest of the Chief, after we had gone through an entire week of tittle-tattle, small talk, and sensationalism. The news that a Child Jesus had disappeared from the National Exposition of Popular and Native Art presented by the National Institute of Arts, Sciences, and Letters (or, to put it in fewer words, by Tuto Ramírez) ran through the city like a dust devil, and, of course made newspaper headlines immediately. Of course, the kidnapping was discovered at once. How could it be otherwise? I think that the exposition consisted of only twenty-eight objects of its kind, entrusted to the custody of the museum: among them, nine Infants Jesus in the cradle, three sets of Wise Men, four Christs, a like number of Virgins, and the remainder saints chosen at random. All of the images were of local handicraft; that is, they were the work of clever agricultural laborers who kill time and while away their enforced idleness during the rainy season by carving those figurines out of soft wood with a jackknife. I must confess that to me they seem like a lot of junk, though nowadays people have taken it into their heads to admire them with uncomprehending eyes.

"Well, as I say, the kidnapping of the Christ Child was discovered immediately. And, into the bargain, it was not long before the name of the abductor was known. What made the case ticklish is that the kidnapper was not a man likely to be suspected, not one of the schoolchildren who were made to stand in line for the exposition, not a common thief, not even such a known kleptomaniac as Don Serafín Lovera, upon whom suspicion instantly fell, but—who would have thought it?—one of our national leading lights: the poet and academy member, Carmelo Zapata. I never could determine how he was found out. The only thing I know is that the rumor proved true, for when the outcry was taken up by the public and grew so clamorous that no one could ignore it, the famous poet appeared voluntarily near closing time at the place where the exposition was being held, carrying a mysterious little package in one hand. He asked for the secretary, and, after shutting himself up with Tuto in the latter's office, solemnly handed him what turned out to be, not precisely the image that had been snatched, but a very fine Infant Jesus done in plaster of Paris and lying on a cradle of cleverly painted straw, which he explained had been bought by him at the shop where religious articles are sold as a substitute for that grotesque figurine, as he called it, that he had felt in duty bound to retire from the exposition as a token protest,

[76]

motivated solely by reverence and a regard for public decency, and thus withdraw it from the innocent eyes of our modest young ladies and matrons, as well as from those of the tender school children, *et cetera, et cetera.*

"The garrulousness of the great bard, never chary of words, already is well known. That was his explanation for his act; he had done it out of reverence and a regard for public decency. Not until later would those motives of his come to light. Tuto Ramírez, with more than every right, considering his position as secretary of the exposition, refused for the moment to make himself responsible for the substitute Child Jesus, on the ground that the figurine, however pretty and pleasant and perfect it might be, was, after all, the product of modern industry designed to please the religious taste of our day, and could not by any means take the place there of a little work, modest if you like, but of pure popular inspiration. He declared emphatically that its value resided precisely in the crude candor of an unknown artist, a humble exponent of the temperament of the race. Then Carmelo, who had his own temperament, grew very angry, and seems to have told Tuto, his eyes flaming with a dark fury, that the only thing that kept him from smashing the Infant Jesus over his head or shoving it in his face was respect for what it represented. But, in any event, he made it known that under no circumstances did he intend to return that shameful blasphemy. 'All right, whatever you wish, Don Carmelo,' Tuto answered, white with rage. 'I shall consider that I have done my duty by taking the case to the highest echelons.' With great dignity he then began to arrange the papers on his desk, thus indicating that he would take no more notice of the poet's presence. The latter, equally dignified, went out, slamming the door.

"Of course Tuto Ramírez lost no time in going to the highest echelons with his case. Indeed, the highest echelons, evil intentioned, conferred upon his Minister of Public Instruction, Don Luisito Rosales, the task of dealing with it and rescuing the kidnapped work of art. Every time the Chief sent out a special call for his minister, that poor creature would enter the Presence half terrified. 'What's it all about?' he asked me as he passed my desk in the anteroom, and I, with all due respect, played my usual joke by passing the thumb of my right hand around my throat, meaning off with his head. Then with the same thumb, I pointed to His Excellency's door and, following the Chief's instructions, trailed into the salon after him. When my Don Luisito heard about the task the President was entrusting to him, he calmed down at first, then gave a start. 'I?' he protested, in alarm. Bocanegra answered him with great forebearance. 'Of course you. If not you, who then, Mr. Minister? You, Doctor, must find out for me whatever it was that induced the Heavenly Poetaster to perpetrate his theft, and then it'll be up to you to persuade him that he must return the little sacred image to us for the good of the fatherland. After that, we'll drop it as only a joke.' 'Very well, very well; but you know, Chief, how Carmelo carries on; you are not unaware that the great bard does not handle matters in any too subtle a manner when politeness is called for. He's going to deny it, for he's excessively arrogant, and he'll end up by being very disrespectful to me . . .' Don Luisito was trying to cover his reluctance with a half-jesting tone. 'Oh, no, no he won't; he won't do that ever,' the president exclaimed deliberately. 'If anything like that should happen, which I don't believe, you, Doctor, can threaten him with taking the case to court, as a criminal action, and you'll see that the bard will climb down off his high horse right away. Yes, my dear Doctor, he'll back down, believe me, you need have no doubt about that. Besides,' he concluded, 'you can take Tadeo Requena with you. He's young and strong. Just in case. You heard me,' he added, addressing me now. 'You're to go with the doctor.'

"What he really wanted was to have someone there who could describe the scene to him, for his own enjoyment, and give him a laugh. He was promising himself a delicious morsel, following the *antipasto* that Tuto Ramírez had described to him in detail. And who would be a better witness than I, his faithful secretary? Up to then, my dealings with Carmelo Zapata could have been boiled down to almost nothing, although his name, his personality, and renown had been known to me since the days of my paradisiacal literary innocence, when the Galician, Luna, in San

Cosme had lent me the back numbers of the Sunday *El Comercio* for my solace and recreation, as he put it.

"Later, in the capital, during the period when I was a student, Don Luisito Rosales, doubtless judged that to meet the great bard whose verses I had brought with me and already had learned in the village, would make a potent contribution to my education. So he sent me to pay him a visit one day, after making previous arrangements by telephone and citing the keen interest that would accrue to me at a time when he himself was striving to make a useful citizen of me in short order. I am not ashamed of the ingenuous thrill I felt later as I approached the sanctuary of the muses. Carmelo Zapata was somebody. After keeping me waiting a reasonably short time, he received me seated in front of his writing desk with his pen at the ready, between the gleaming plaster cast of a Nike of Samothrace to his right, and the famous artistic ashtray, decorated with a Don Quixote on horseback, which the ladies of the Pedagogical Atheneum had conferred upon him on the recent and memorable occasion of his golden wedding to poetry, so fitly celebrated all over the country. The bard received me benevolently, after a cough from me had drawn him forth from the meditation into which he had sunk. He was affable, paternal toward me, and in a few well-chosen phrases he enlightened me regarding the importance of the role played by the poet in society, whose greatest exponent he is through the spirit and the word. 'Unhappy the people,' he declaimed, 'unhappy the nations who cannot recognize, honor, and venerate their bards.'

" 'And is that all that Carmelo taught you?' Dr. Rosales asked later, when I told him about the interview. He never sent me to that house again, and he chose—greatly pleased in his heart— to instruct me in *belles-lettres* himself, with all their Greek and Latin make-weights. Now, years later, Bocanegra was ordering me to contend with the bard over the exacerbating subject of the Infant Jesus, both lost and found in his power, merely for the sake of amusing himself over the imbroglio, and of sending me to be his private witness, narrator, and chronicler.

"But in the end, the spectacle turned out not to be as amusing as His Excellency had promised himself it would. First of all, poor Don Luisito let the entire day go by without taking any forethought, and did not start the fearful operation until the following day, when he put the telephone wire between his timid face and the bard's big snout. He said that he had heard of the incident concerning the exposition and that he would be very grateful if, whenever it might be most convenient to him, the bard would take a little stroll around to his office and they would try to find a friendly solution to the problem. The poet, to whom the Infant Jesus had become a hot potato that he had to keep juggling between his hands, turned up in person immediately, this time carrying not one but two little packages, which when he entered he set down together upon the desk where I was writing or pretending to write when he arrived. Apparently he was in a mood to compromise; his attitude was conciliatory, or so it seemed at first glance. He explained that during his visit to the exposition, he had suffered an actual shock when he realized the indecency with which the Infant Jesus had been represented in one of those images, and that, consequently, not at all surreptitiously—to say that was a vile calumny—but ostentatiously rather, and openly, as the fact that everyone found out about it would serve to demonstrate, he had taken possession of the sacrilegious image and . . . 'Well, let us see the *quid*. What was it all about? Let us determine the reason once and for all,' Dr. Rosales urged him.

"Then our man, without another word, unwrapped one of the two little packages he had left on my desk and, when he had uncovered it (it was the stolen Infant, of course), said, 'See, Mr. Minister, this is the *quid*.' He stepped back waiting in a triumphant and, inwardly, a somewhat uneasy expectancy. Don Luisito put on his spectacles, studied the object and, after observing it for a moment or two, asked, 'What's so special about that? To be sure, it's not very pretty. It's a crude little piece of junk, but no different from the others, no better and no worse.'

"Through that silence, that atmosphere, I could sense the embarrassed indignation of the poet Carmelo. He turned to me (I was still pretending to be busy with my own work) and appealed to me: 'Come here, young man, as a favor to me, for the minister is half blind. Look at it with your own eyes.' I went up to the image, toward which Zapata was now pointing. The poet's finger was aiming rigidly at the crotch of the naked Infant. I must admit that in fact, that *thing* was a little exaggerated, indeed quite exaggerated. The figurine had been blessed, not by Nature, but by the imagination of its artificer, with an overlarge attribute of virility, whereas it should have been kept down to a mere hint of a promise for its tender age, rather than being displayed with such mature realism. 'Ah, that!' the doctor exclaimed, and at the same time I burst out laughing. To be sure the rustic sculptor's jackknife had come against a knot in the wood there, and he had chosen to sin on the side of too much instead of too little. But the bard was highly indignant, all the more so because of my laughter and the minister's feeble reaction. 'You must realize,' he argued, resorting to reasonableness, 'that this is intolerably irreverent, and that I, as a good Catholic, am not prepared to countenance it. That was why I carried the thing home, and then, lest anyone take it in bad part or suspect me of a covetous interest in it, or be given grounds to talk about theft—such stupidity! —I bought this other image to donate to the museum as a gift.' At this point, while he was speaking, he slipped out the enchanting, blessed Infant Jesus acquired in the religious articles store. Its fat little hand was extended in a blessing, and its little belly delicately covered with a scarf.

" 'Well, I'm very sorry, my illustrious friend, believe me; I regret it with all my heart, but the exchange you are proposing cannot be accepted, owing to the notoriety this matter has attained. And permit me to reproach you for having acted in this same matter with excessive haste and a lack of premeditation.' It was evident that Dr. Rosales was measuring his words, and he refused to meet the bard's eyes. But I was noticing from Carmelo Zapata's face that in spite of so much punctilio, the decision was poison to our poet laureate, who was turning ashy. 'Your objection,' the doctor went on, 'your objection to that image is, of course, most praiseworthy, though, to tell the truth, I am unable to find any wrong intention in it, but instead a lack of skill in the man who carved it. But, in any case, you might write a discreet letter to the secretary of the institute, and to me, also, and together we . . .' 'So,' interrupted the bard in a burst of arrogance, 'so, to top it all off, you go so far as to call me indiscreet. That was all that was lacking,' he shouted, furious, his eyes turning bloodshot. 'Well, let me tell you, Sir Minister, that you will have to answer to me for that insult on the field of honor. I shall send you my seconds.'

"Impelled by curiosity, I turned to observe the reaction of my Don Luisito to such an outburst, and I noted that after his initial dismay, he drew himself up with a hitherto unknown flash of anger in his eyes. But it was only a spark; instantly he replied in a light, familiar, and extremely pacifying tone, 'See here, Carmelo, you listen to me. Don't be stupid.'

"That was something I would never have expected. One has dealings with a person time after time, but no one ever knows what each man carries concealed in his secret places. Carmelo lowered his eyes to the floor, from where his oxfords were shining up at him, and he let more than a little time go by before making up his mind to say no more. The first thing he said, spoken in a voice half regretful, half reflective, was, 'Well, this can't be left like this. If you will not answer my challenge, I shall have to challenge Tuto Ramírez.' "

CHAPTER

12

++++++++++++++++++++++++++++

I am becoming aware that I have fallen behind a little in the flow of those blessed memoirs, without any rhyme or reason, and that I have wandered away from the plan of my notes, which is merely to gather and evaluate critically the documents at my disposal so that someday I may write the history of our present disasters with a clearer mind. If the excerpts I have just extracted serve any purpose, it is to throw into bold relief the atmosphere of obsequience, servility, and grotesque debasement to which Antón Bocanegra's regime had brought us, and at the same time to sketch in outline the moral portrait of the tyrant, with, as a by-product, that of this private secretary, who was to murder him.

After digressing this much, I do not wish to pass over a detail that I am personally interested in picking up so as to establish certain essential accounts as circumstantial evidence for the future. This has to do with a conversation, not to say an argument, which took place at one of the First Lady's parties, concerning the widely discussed article by Camarasa on "How A Nation Is Made." This article was the genesis of a small scandal in its day, a mere *scandalette* of little consequence. Rather I should say of little immediate consequence, for in time it was to have remote and very serious and irreparable consequences for its author. Who doesn't remember that wretched screed? It was an insolent piece, aimed at burlesquing and sweeping away our patriotic sentiments and fostering skepticism with regard to the values of the kind that it is not sensible to place under scrutiny. There the article is, then, in the back numbers of *El Comercio,* for whoever may have the curiosity to look it up for the doubtful pleasure of running through it again.

As for me, I recall its terms very well indeed. Camarasa was professing to reveal in the form of a dream his patriotic zeal as an Almerían (for our man was a native of that God-forsaken, dry, and disgruntled Andalusian province whose sons seek their daily bread as a rule in the north of Africa, forced to emigrate by their poverty). He was assuming in fancy that as the outgrowth of an alleged incident with Morocco stirred up by the question of sovereignty over Ceuta and Melilla, a Mussulman landing had been made on the shores of Almería, followed by the declaration of independence of that ancient Moslem kingdom, which was again affirming itself a state independent of Spain. That ridiculous plot gave Camarasa an opportunity to jeer at everyone simultaneously, and especially at the struggles that must be made by a small, young nation like ours—by laboriously gleaning from the past—to compile a solid mass of traditions for itself, traditions at least presentable, if not glorious, from which the citizens can derive pride, the political orators an arsenal of sure-fire themes, and the schoolteachers a set of examples worthy of emulation.

Later the editor-in-chief of *El Comercio* attested that he had sent the article to press without reading it, all in good faith, and unawares, and with some sort of notion that it probably treated some routine or innocuous theme. To the contrary, it turned out to be a time bomb.

Certainly it was all of that! More so than anyone could have guessed. For a time it awakened no repercussions whatsoever, neither on the day following its publication nor on the day after that. The first to react was the Minister Plenipotentiary of Spain, who, as later became known, discreetly alerted the Secretary of State by calling to his attention the bad effect such jokes could produce and pointing out that they could lead to nothing but needless worries and the creation of an atmosphere of insecurity concerning Spanish international policy from which Communism alone would benefit. Furthermore, he regretted—I am speaking of the diplomat—that any compatriot of his could descend to such sneers, however well concealed, at the expense of the country that so generously and cheerfully had offered him asylum. An attitude like that can only give the lie to, sully, and discredit the concept of the proverbial Spanish nobility of character. Three days later *El Diario Ilustrado* finally came out with an unsigned release, under the title "Almería Is Not America, Nor Are We Fools," manfully refuting the insults with which a certain individual had permitted himself to make a mock of even the purest of patriotic sentiments, thereby abusing our country's generous but, let us face it, somewhat senseless hospitality. Other indignant attacks upon the hapless pamphleteer followed that one. Among them the note inserted in the *Army and National Police Bulletin* under the headline "He Must Think He's A Wit" was outstanding for its vitriolic virulence.

At this point, it is to my interest to clarify matters. For Tadeo declares, though merely in passing, that everyone agreed upon attributing it to me—to that tadpole of a Little Pinedo, as the barefaced rascal puts it. And as it would appear that the attribution of that provenance of the said note also was circulated through the conversations in the palace, which he recounts, it would avail me little to try now to suppress the corresponding passage in the memoirs. For even though Tadeo and several of the persons then present have vanished, such things remain. People still talk, comment, conjecture, and avow, until what was rumor has come to be an article of faith. All that would matter little to me if it were not that now trouble is again piled on trouble, and I know and I realize that during these present

[85]

days plenty of people have started saying again that I was also the one who informed on Camarasa, thus providing with an excuse those who wanted him assassinated. Accordingly, I would rather take the bull by the horns and have things clarified once and for all, let the chips fall where they may. I will not deny therefore that it was I who wrote the note in the *Army and National Police Bulletin*. Someone had to bar the way to that reckless man, someone had to dot the *i*'s and cross the *t*'s so as to leave no room for doubt. At that party presided over by Doña Concha this was unanimously recognized. And that someone was I, though it might have been anyone else.

Actually, I did not write the note on my own initiative. I did it at the behest of my uncle, the late General Malagarriga, then Secretary of War, who wanted to provide me with an opportunity to earn a pinch from the fund administered by Old Olóriz at the same time. I feel sure that my uncle would not have acted in this instance without at least a nod from his commander-in-chief, the worthy president of the nation. And to judge by what Requena tells us, the Chief must have found it very pleasant then to show how magnanimous he was toward those who were condemning the "venomous" tone of the note, but only so that he could range himself on the side opposite that of his dearly beloved spouse. His Excellency even went so far as to opine that no one but a character like me, embittered by misfortune, could distill so much cold poison into so few lines. She, on the other hand, was so furious at the barefaced impudence of the Spanish scribbler that any punishment whatsoever would not have seemed enough to her. She compared my note with the article by Camarasa and found that it was the only adequate reply.

I was pleased to discover, moreover, that the president's wife was not the only defender of my diatribe. That wretch of a Camarasa had contrived to write his article in such a way as to annoy everyone for one reason or another, and he had laid himself open to the most diverse interpretations by his ambiguity, most of them absurd, I grant you. Nearly all of the allusions and parallels he was pretending to disclose had to be dragged in almost by the hair of the head. Some people even ventured a guess that the libel had been brewed in the Spanish legation, as a sneer at our country, and that the protest of the Minister Plenipotentiary was a kind of alibi, which served only to countersink the nail. This nonsense, like all the other nonsense, reached the streets later and was widely circulated there, and it could be traced—at least so everyone was given to understand—to the muse of Carmelo Zapata, who was highly enraged, I'm sure I don't know why, by the facetious remarks of Camarasa concerning the Almerían poet, Francisco Villaespesa, whom he characterized in his article as the glorious troubador of the New World, whose birthplace, owing to poetic licence, was given as the still unredeemed territory of Almería. "Some more of Carmelo's stupid nonsense," Bocanegra pronounced it peremptorily as he tossed a drink down his throat. "And if you should see," he added, "that, in spite of everything, Camarasa's article amused me."

This was the final word, a grant of absolution. Meanwhile Camarasa was left quite unperturbed by all the commotion. He remained quite unperturbed for the time being, I should say. No one could have imagined what was to happen later. The time bomb, temporarily forgotten, ended by killing the man who had put it together. But why should I blame myself for that, by what rule of three can they involve me in this? If we spin it out fine, we are all to blame for whatever happens in the world, and some responsibility falls upon all of us, willy-nilly. It would be funny if it should happen now that I . . .

13

++++++++++++++++++++++++++++++

The situation of our country under the Bocanegra government was very bad, as bad as could be. Had it not been for his demagoguery, we might not have sunk to where we are now. But if we raise our eyes toward that tyrant from the deep hole we are in, his image is now almost confused with that of the good things lost. So relative are the things of this world. In the midst of so much ignominy, there was always someone then to come to our rescue, to hold out a hand, if a hand was needed.

Far be it from me to defend or to excuse in any way the president's lady, Doña Concha. No one could deny that a great part of the odium that accumulated around Bocanegra's figure over the years had been engendered by her, his wife. But the unhappy woman has come to a terrible end now; her sins, which were in no sense venial, though their depths are still generally unknown hereabouts, have brought her the cruelest punishment. Poor

First Lady, flung from the eminence of a capricious and limitless power into that inhuman imprisonment in the Immaculate Lady, where every kind of torment and misery awaited her before death came for her at the hands of an idiot. *Requiescat!* She was frivolous, she was ambitious, she was arbitrary, she was mad. Her overbearing manner, her insatiable thirst to prevail, to impose her will, to demand, to dispose, and to shine in her dealings with the very people who went to her seeking protection or connivance irritated them.

But for all that, there was something generous in her violence; her blind passion did not lack a certain grandeur, and I remember that in the incident having to do with my attack on Camarasa in the *Army and National Police Bulletin* she defended me without reservation after her husband had taken it into his head to side with the insufferable Spanish journalist out of sheer bad blood. Who would defend me now if, to mention an example, I should one day be accused of having had him assassinated? Later, after my uncle, poor Antenor, had passed on to a better life, the friendship between his widow, the absurd Loreto, and the First Lady, even constituted a continuing peace bond for me, up to a point. Up to a point, I say, for it is one thing to be the nephew of General Antenor Malagarriga, the Secretary of War, and another to depend upon a female filled with resentment toward all his political bedfellows, and mentally unbalanced in the bargain.

Antenor's sudden death left me dismayed, as can well be imagined, and without a clue to whatever disagreeable repercussions it might have on me. For the time being I abstained, out of prudence, from seeking very much contact with his widow. I had never had much sympathy for Loreto, and she could hardly have failed to notice it. On the other hand, I paid increasingly frequent visits to that doddering Old Olóriz, her relative and guardian. I could find ample grounds for pressing my contacts with him, for he had seen fit to make me a more or less regular allowance from the funds allotted to him, in payment for this or that idea. Accordingly, there was no reason why I should not drop by his house almost without calculation, through sheer instinct— he did all the work of his office at home—and even be persuaded to stay there playing cards with him into the small hours of the night. Perhaps for the very reason that I never wearied of helping him to pass away his sleepless hours, Old Olóriz kept the bread box half-way open for me. He could arrange to assign me a fee, under the heading of Special and Reserved Services, always provided that it was done with discretion. For my part, what choice did I have? I had to go on living, didn't I? Besides, Olóriz and I were related in a way, and kindly disposed toward each other. I was the nephew of the late General Malagarriga; he was the uncle of Loreto, the general's widow.

It was Olóriz who told me one day about the kind of mental imbalance that had taken possession of her, a strange obsession, which I was later to experience directly, adorned with infinite proliferations, from the lips of the lady in question. The good *señora* claimed that she had been favored with a revelation, no less. According to her hallucinations, on the day following the patriotic celebrations on the famous 28th of February, also the occasion of their silver wedding anniversary, they had planned to hold an intimate little celebration for close friends. In making preparations for it, she, Loreto, be it said parenthetically, had had to work like a donkey, and Antenor had tippled prodigally, of course, so as not to slight custom. Well, then, when the last of the guests finally had left and she could go to bed exhausted, a very strange dream came to her. She dreamed that her husband . . . Only it was not Antenor. No, no, it was not that Antenor, with his absent voice and somewhat antipathetic person, but a wondrous Presence ("Wondrous, I assure you of that," she would ponder in telling of it, "something like a resplendant Sacred Heart, or the Archangel Gabriel, or that Buddha, almost adolescent, about whom I read something in a novel a short while ago"). In short, a Presence who was Antenor and yet not he, and who made an address to her that she still was able to recall word for word. He had said to her, "Loreto, for twenty-five years, I have stood at your side in the capacity of husband without your ever having recognized me or being aware of who I am. That is the reason—and it will be well for you to know it—that I have never given you the son you longed for. On my return from my group meeting every Saturday, I have fulfilled my conjugal duties to you with soldierly punctuality—yes, during all that not inconsiderable lapse of time, as you well know. In spite of that, you customarily accepted my virile loyalties with faint enthusiasm, more often than not amid yawns and groans of protest. But what fruit did they bear? None! And now it is all over; the test has been conclusive. Before parting from you forever, I shall not leave your side without telling you who I am." After such a queer pronouncement as that, the marvelous Presence had leaned down to her ear, and with unmistakable clarity and precision had pronounced a name, only to vanish instantly. But, alas, that name, which had been like a radiance at that moment, like a very clear, sweet flash of light, had been wiped forthwith from her memory, probably owing to her astonishment, her perturbation, and what came immediately afterward. So that, although it was the key word, it was also the one word lost from the entire address.

Never, never again had she succeeded in recapturing it. At that moment she awakened in intense agitation. Her heart seemed ready to jump out of her mouth. There were tears in her eyes; her throat felt constricted. She awakened and turned over in bed in a frenzy to embrace her husband, that marvelous and fugitive Presence, for the delightful yet comfortless revelation that he had just made to her. But the horrible fact is that though Antenor was at her side, he lay there inert and cold. He was a corpse, as the newspapers later emphasized in a feeling obituary notice. He had been the victim of a heart attack, as the authorities duly certified. At the very moment when she was lighting the night lamp, the terrified *señora* was able to take in nothing but that the man there at her side (Presence or no Presence) was nothing but a vulgar falsification, a mockery, a base lie, a travesty of the Antenor she knew, the bore with the limp moustache and a kind of clownish rictus on his face. After such a shock, how could she remember the delicious name that had been whispered in her ear?

"Imagine the efforts of concentration I have made since then to remember the mysterious name. At times, I can feel it approach a corner of my mind, I have it on the tip of my tongue, as the saying goes. I feel it, I hear it as if muted, but in the end am never able to make it out. Nothing! It never comes after all. Believe me, I could weep with desperation. I swear that I can never die happy until I can hear that voice at least once more and see that spirit, which lived with me so many years without my suspecting it. And to think that he, the wretch, never let me know about him until the very end! Why did he do that to me? I never lose the hope . . ."

Loreto herself said that to me some time later, during the period of the great spiritualistic séances, when she was installed in the National Palace, aiding and abetting the affair between her friend, the First Lady, and Private Secretary Requena, lending them her bedroom for their clandestine turtledove grapplings and keeping watch for them at the door. That sort of unqualified and loyal friendship between women always has seemed remarkable to me. It seems to league them against the world. No doubt it is damnable, but at the same time there is something moving about it. No considerations of self-interest, of principle, no other duties, affections, or obligations are strong enough to break up such alliances, which will explode, and with what violence, only if the Devil has enmeshed them in some web of passion! No such nasty trick ever had been played on Doña Concha, the president's wife, and Loreto. They never had found themselves at sword's point in a conflict of that kind, and thus their friendship did indeed last as long as they lived—that is to say until the death of the president's wife—and even after, as we shall see when the time comes. But I'd better not run ahead of my story.

CHAPTER

14

++++++++++++++++++++++++++++

After the solemn obsequies pronounced over my Uncle Antenor and his burial, it was said that Doña Concha had had his widow, her inseparable Loreto, moved into the palace to live with her. The two ladies were united in a *prehistoric* friendship, as they used to call it, alluding to the time when neither of them had yet met her future spouse. They had never even dreamed then that in the course of time they would find themselves moved up, the one to the generalship, the other to the presidency. Their fortunes had changed at almost the same time, and how amazingly; and on the higher plane where they then moved, their friendship endured, unalterable, solidified, and so much richer in fertile possibilities. Thus, when Bocanegra climbed to the dignity of chief of state, the gaudy First Lady of the Republic and her friend, Loreto, then the lawful wife of General Malagarriga, schemed to have my unhappy uncle appointed to the cabinet. Loreto won poor Antenor over, and Doña Concha did her part by going to work on Bocanegra. And so it was that one of the old-time generals began by his collaboration to support, guarantee, and lend prestige to the Father of the Poor and his abominable regime. I feel sure that among the satisfactions garnered by that woman, who was my aunt whether I liked it or not, one of the greatest was that of annoying us, her in-laws, whom she detested *en masse* beyond a shadow of a doubt. Well she knew that nothing could annoy us so much as Antenor's new turn on top of everything else. And yet . . .

As was quite natural, he later took advantage of the influence he thus acquired, using it to find good positions for his people, beginning with that repulsive Olóriz, who before Loreto's marriage to General Malagarriga had never even been suspected to have such a niece, though earlier he had already obtained, no one quite knew how, the post of Civil Adjustor, settling questions of extra pay, *per diems,* and provisions for army personnel below the rank of captain. The later post, which was now obtained for him—Administrator of Special and Reserve Services—was more remunerative and no less discreet. By their very nature, the funds at his disposal were exempt from fiscal audits and therefore, in effect, could be drawn upon. Consequently the venerable old gentleman used to entertain himself in passing with the practice of usury, and he used up all his mental energy at that time by combining his tasks with card games.

One thing must be granted to Loreto: her new position did not go to her head, nor did she feel any vertigo in the rarefied air, as the First Lady did. In the final analysis she cannot be called a bad person, and the way she has behaved and is behaving in these times of misfortune after so much good fortune has reconciled me to her. If she was able to hoodwink my uncle Antenor by her intrigues, that was an enterprise that did not call for the talents of an Aspasia, for the poor man never would have been conspicuous for his acuity, or his brilliance, or his *brio,* or his exquisite sensibility, or for any other quality that would lift him above the common level. But when it came to being a good man, he was all of that, as good as gold, an excellent person, whose weaknesses ought to be overlooked. Yet the mere fact of his having chosen as consort a woman of Loreto's physical and spiritual type marks him, I think, and colors his whole being. As I was saying, then, she did in fact hoodwink him, and inveigle him, and drag him into contracting a lawful marriage. It is no less true, however, that, once her objective had been achieved and she finally had calmed down, she applied herself to serving her fellowman with all the resources of her scanty wits. With all that, it is a well-known fact that good will badly directed usually turns into an instrument for blameworthy ends, and Loreto, with her melancholy mania about the marvelous Presence, but also with all the shrewdness of an artful woman, unfortunately still acted during that entire period as her friend's good right hand.

At that time Doña Concha was riding high and unbridled; those were the years of her apogee. Bocanegra was at the peak of his power, and his wife was introducing the notes of eccentricity and adding her ludicrous touches to the scandal of his tyranny. Perhaps because crime makes itself respected, even in a sinister fashion, the atrocities imputed to that complete rascal failed to arouse as much indignation as the brain storms and caprices, the arrogant frivolity exhibited by that woman. To accept and suffer her didoes doubtless was more humiliating than to succumb to physical fear, and awakened a greater animosity; but, at the same time, the picturesque, even grotesque character of each new episode of hers offered splendid fodder to the devouring idleness and boredom of the social gatherings and provided backbiters with the delicious revenge of ridicule. By such means, anger was dissipated; and meanwhile the usual portrait of the First Lady was primarily that of a vain prima donna, arbitrary and heedless, but also with traces of libidinousness. And to the vast consternation of those who could not stomach the regime, most people considered excusable and predictable, even ultimately insignificant, not only the presence of her intimate pal, Loreto, but also her complicity, both passive and active, strange as it may seem!

In short, she granted herself satisfactions that would not be permitted a royal princess; and to avoid wandering off into generalities, I shall cite only the episode involving Fanny, the famous Japanese bitch, whose pawprints must still be in the archives of the United States State Department, and even of the War Office, for without the benevolent intervention of the United States ambassador, our First Lady might never have been enabled to console herself for the death of her adored pet, a wretched little animal with enormous bat ears, but a purebred, rare, expensive, very delicate, fragile, unbelievable, gentle little creature that was her ornament, love, and delight, and whose tender little soul departed this vale of tears and flew straight to Heaven at the end of one heart-breaking day. A time of national mourning was all but declared. The demise of this "enchanting and most intelligent dog" was a news item for press and radio. The inconsolability into which the sad event had thrown the noble matron was mentioned, and television offered the public an old photograph showing Doña Concha, smiling and happy, with Fanny in her arms. The proper sort of elegy or lyrical epitaph appeared, too, the work of the indefatigable poet, Carmelo Zapata, published in the Sunday literary supplement of *El Comercio,* framed in a discreet black border. And, of course, in the face of such a mani- festation of public sorrow, the members of the diplomatic corps could hardly be guilty of lack of feeling. Each of them took the first available opportunity to express his condolences to the *señora.* But this time the truly delicate touch was the work, not of the representative of Her Britannic Majesty, nor of the en- voy from the Mother Country, nor of the sentimental Italian ambassador, nor of the cultivated Frenchman, not to speak of the gentlemen from the sister republics, but—who would have thought it?—of the Colossus of the North. Yes, of Mr. Grogg, who, deeply touched by the First Lady's carryings-on, promised to try to find for her forthwith another little bitch identical with the deceased. Seemingly, a creature of that breed is not easily come by, and only in the United States, where nothing is lacking, could one like it be obtained. Indeed they brought her in a United States Army airplane, from which Fanny *rediviva* emerged, a glorious substitute, a few days after the interment.

A lot of nonsense, agreed; and when all is said and done of

no importance whatsoever in comparison with the wantonness to which the First Lady gave herself over in private, and especially with the conspiracy in which she finally involved Tadeo Requena by thrusting him into the perpetration of a deed whose consequences were to prove fatal to them both and to the entire country. The case of the little Japanese bitch does not go beyond a somewhat inoffensive indication of her thirst for being conspicuous and overbearing; and if it was so much talked about, that was only because frivolity is precipitated in a chemically pure state here, and additionally because the *gringos,* whose mere existence generally is a cause for indignation among us these days, had become involved. Naturally, the most implacable censure was directed toward the Colossus of the North, and with every reason. Some people are incapable of imagining how offensive their ill-conceived gestures of friendship sometimes can turn out to be.

To complete the case, let us turn to the version that the Spanish minister submitted in one of his regular reports. In his somewhat pompous style, he duly relates to the authorities the story of the death of the little Japanese grayhound, the property of the wife of the Chief of State; a trifling event, he says, which nonetheless has not failed to have repercussions worth taking into account. "The reigning atmosphere of adulation here is such," he adds, "that a domestic occurrence like that can go beyond publicity to acquire incredible proportions; and, in that atmosphere of general hysteria (the mere fact that a radio speaker announced the news in a voice so choked that he seemed on the verge of bursting into tears will give Your Excellency some notion of it), the dean of the diplomatic corps felt obligated to convene us in order to take official notice of it. The only rational decision was reached: that each might let a kind word fall in the lady's ear at his own discretion, but without any official character whatsoever.

"The action of the United States ambassador reached the limit within the framework of this agreement. Your Excellency already knows through earlier reports the ingenuous nature of Mr. Grogg, and how he tries to follow the rules for winning friends laid down by his government with regard to the Latin American countries.

This time the man thought that he had scored a triumph by making the *señora* the gift of a bitch of the same breed. And, as if that were not enough, he brought it in a military air transport plane, doubtless with the intention of 'tightening the bonds of friendship that unite the republics of the American continent,' as some newspaperman here put it in his news story. Obviously, the *señora* feels highly flattered. But I doubt that the president himself, a sagacious enough man, though impenetrable, will allow himself to be impressed by such crude diplomacy, which in the end would never suffice to counterbalance the undeviating love the Latin American people bear the Mother Country."

Assuredly the Spanish minister did not go far afield in this summation; for Bocanegra's private secretary himself confirms it—irrefutable testimony—when, as might have been foreseen, he echoes the much-bruited affair in his memoirs. Tadeo tells here that his master asked him on his own initiative in a half absent-minded voice as he was signing some papers: "What did you think of Mr. Grogg's gesture?" In line with Requena's sly custom, he abstained from answering until His Excellency pressed him, still not looking at him. "What do you think? How much would a little beast like that cost?" Then he ventured a guess. "The United States Treasury certainly must have paid for the whole thing." It appears that he added two or three more remarks, half groaning as he smudged the papers with the ash from his eternal cigar, until finally the young secretary commented, for the sake of saying something: "And they brought it in an army Superfortress." Whereupon Bocanegra again pressed the point: "A dog can't cost very much, can it?"

Doña Concha, on the other hand, was enchanted; Tadeo also tells us that. She conferred the title of "my friend" upon Grogg, and every time the poor fellow went to the palace, he was forced to be the recipient of the new Fanny's friendly attentions. "As for me," the secretary writes, "I'd give I don't know what to see the poor slob, blushing and smiling and turning away his face as that stupid bitch persists in bussing him with her wet little rat's snout."

CHAPTER

15

✦✦✦✦✦✦✦✦✦✦✦✦✦✦✦✦✦✦✦✦✦✦✦✦✦

I keep asking myself whether I am doing right in spreading myself so wide and in recounting such nonsense in so much detail as I sit here with my door locked while the main actors in the story have died by violence and the people outside still are killing one another, so that each of our lives literally hangs by a thread. I keep asking myself whether such trivia are even worth recording as history. But on careful thought, I think they are. Given the background of the situation unleashed by such follies, anecdotes like the one about Fanny acquire a tragic significance. Frivolity may attain the dimensions of tragedy; it may have the effect of a slap in the face or of being spat upon.

It must be understood that I am not going to cite the endless situations in which that woman's vanity operated disguised as cultural activities, social policy, beneficence—this, that, or the other activity designed to deceive some of the people. I have selected the above case because it reveals so much in all its nakedness—and, to boot, such obscene nakedness that the taunts of the respectable public (I remember well the evaluations poured out in my group at the Aurora) concerning the bitchiness of little Fanny were unanimously extended to her owner. The biggest bitch of all was the invariable refrain of each new remark. And of course she was the biggest! Just to look at her was enough: her poses, her way of looking at you, her somewhat husky voice, her loud laugh, her dress, her mere presence added up to lewdness and aroused an aggressive concupiscence in men. But all this would have been nothing if it had been only that. The truly explosive factor in her personality was the mingling of such lewdness with ambition. Without that last very powerful ingredient, her tricks or her dissipations would not have gone beyond the category of venial sin; what aggravated those sins was that they were combined with an almost compulsive urgency to intrigue, to scheme, and to plot unceasingly, so that what might otherwise have been called her weaknesses became transmuted into forces, and demoniac forces at that. To her the casting of her nets and catching everyone in them was a sport. I do not believe that she laid her plans with any clear objective in view; very likely her designs were sketched or outlined as simple phenomena of the process of weaving and unweaving, like caprices cast aside and soon forgotten. Or it may be that they acquired an obsessive fixity, in which case they became so obscure in process that she herself became entangled in her own net in the end.

I suspect that something of that sort happened during her intrigue with the secretary, Requena, in the course of which she used her *prehistoric* friend Loreto as her accomplice and cover. That imbecile would have backed her blindly in any case, and the other crafty one would not even have needed to exploit her delirious mania of the marvelous Presence to lead her into the spiritualistic séances, which she also exploited in order to make a not unwilling tool of young Tadeo. As for him, it is curious that he could be cozened into letting himself be dragged into a guilty liaison that was completely irrational in the bargain and was to prove fatal to everyone in the long run—and not only to them, the authors of the conspiracy, and to the protagonists who played minor roles on the public stage, but also to the entire nation, and even to the wretched historian who is collecting, organizing, and making a fair copy of the present notes. It might be said that our man was the victim of an ineluctable fatality, powerful enough to force him to act in defiance of the strongest propensities of his own character, even against his own instinct, which had made him reluctant.

One is able to infer from his words, as well as from what he does not say in alluding to the thorny subject of his relations with the First Lady of the Republic in the memoirs I have before me, that she was the one who took the initiative; she made all the advances and revealed boundless audacity, while Tadeo, true to his covert tactics as the minion in the palace, confined himself to watching mistrustingly the shape of things to come, always suspicious and coldly calculating, never taking any step whatsoever without first having been, I will not say invited to it, but rather shoved or bullied into it. Before she bullied him into her bed, she must have approached him several times under various pretexts; and after the *consummatum est,* when her sly tricks had accomplished the foreseeable object and they had become each other's prisoner to a certain extent, she did not as his mistress and lady drop even for a moment her maneuvers to make him her creature and to lead him around by the nose.

The group of initiates at the spiritualistic séances, held every Tuesday on the dot under her direction and patronage in a small parlor in the palace, followed wherever she had a notion to lead them. "You'll be dumbfounded," she had assured him, "when you see what kind of people go there; you'll have to come every time from this week on . . ." (He had been resisting—"Especially," he explains, "because I have the inclination, almost the habit, of setting myself against whatever the Big Boss Woman suggests to me. Later I give in. Or I don't give in; it depends. But I always resist in the beginning, as a matter of principle. This time I yielded, thinking that I would meet the archbishop in his mitre, at least. As for the spirits . . .")

Requena's attitude toward the spirits is curious. Actually it does not differ greatly from the one he always maintained toward creatures of flesh and blood, whom he was usually ready to find entirely evil and false. "If I don't meet the spirits, I shall at least meet outstanding people, and I shall treat myself to the pleasure of finding out just what kind of ultratelluric guys such distinguished society has to do with."

The amusing side of the case (and I shall not refrain from stating it in writing, despite its indecency on the ground that after all the *petite histoire* of Cleopatra's nose explains, clarifies, and makes History with a capital letter more comprehensible)— the amusing side of the case, I say, lies in the reason, lightly sketched in outline but surely decisive, why Tadeo showed such unwillingness to attend the spiritualistic meetings in the beginning. His reason was nothing but the fear that Doña Concha would take advantage of the darkness in the room to play a certain kind of joke on him, some tricks that the good woman apparently got special enjoyment out of playing. The secretary states this in his cold, direct, and brutal fashion, but with ill-concealed embarrassment. "By then, all that insistence," he writes, "was irritating me. That woman always thinks she can lead me around wherever she takes a notion to, like a helpless child. And I always felt especially disinclined to have it occur to her to take advantage of the darkness in the room to start handling me beneath the table and thus set my nerves to jangling. She dearly loves to do that. Her manipulations unbeknown to other people amuse her, whether for the thrill of danger or for the loathsome pleasure of trying to arouse me in public, I don't know. But I can't stand it. To me the joke is not at all funny. More than once now I have been forced to push her seeking hand roughly aside in the official automobile, behind the chauffeur's back, to cite one example. But luckily," he adds with relief, "at least she had more respect for the spirits as onlookers, and while they're around she never overstepped the bounds."

I have been unable to withstand the temptation to copy this paragraph here. (Later, when it comes time to prepare the text for publication, we shall see.) With all its grossness, I find it flavorful and expressive. As the headlights of a car may unexpectedly light up an indecorous scene in a corner of some public garden, so those words reveal at a single stroke the character of the *dramatis personae* and the nature of their relationship; and I am not referring to carnal relations so much as to psychological relationship. From the very first moment, young Tadeo always was on the defensive with her. He always distrusted and feared her. Perhaps he detested the destructive element in her personality, though he may not have realized fully where it lay or where the threat was lurking.

I can understand that. I never had any dealings with her other than the superficial and minimal, but indeed I understand perfectly the fear felt by those who came too close to her. Without a doubt she could attract, and at the same time frighten. It has even occurred to me to think. . . After the details my Aunt Loreto has given me concerning her terrible death, I think that terror alone must have been what unleashed the bestiality of that idiot and guided his murderous hand. I can find no other explanation for it; mindless crimes like that are bound to have obscure beginnings, and very simple ones. A wave of panic must have arisen suddenly in the dim mind of that unfortunate fellow when he felt this beautiful woman in his arms, surrounded with an aura of prestige. (The First Lady, she above all!) And to see her smiling at him! And to feel her caressing him! And to know that she was trying to gratify him! Yes, I can easily imagine his fear. Then, terror-stricken, he would grasp the stone fragment and strike her, and strike her, and strike her, until he had crushed her head and obliterated it.

Poor First Lady! Not only toppled from her throne, but also with all control over herself completely lost, she began to employ her customary weapons without rhyme or reason, in such a headless manner, granting her favors to anyone and everyone —to the prison guards, to the first man who solicited them (and in this instance "to solicit" is a euphemism that rings with cruel irony) in a blind search for some sort of protection, her arms threshing desperately like the shipwrecked man in the water who succeeds only in sinking himself ever deeper.

CHAPTER

16

+++++++++++++++++++++++++++

This morning, as I was scanning my papers alone here in my room, I suddenly felt a desire to laugh. It turns out that in this history of ours, which is so steeped in blood, it would seem, as I am documenting it, that the canine race has assigned to itself an almost constant role. Sometimes dogs play the part of buffoons, at other times their parts are highly dramatic, or at least serious. Following the episode of the little bitch, Fanny (to whom no one would deny her historical role, with the intervention of the great world powers and Flying Fortresses in action), another dog must now be assigned a starring role in a certain passage I find in the memoirs of Private Secretary Requena, a passage that I find it indispensable to reproduce in all its fullness, owing to how well it illustrates some of the peculiarities of the environment in which our country's present tragedy was hatched, though of itself it may not have any decisive importance.

I need not underline the cynicism and the insolent masterful-ness that Tadeo boasts about in his account, nor the extreme that the matter went to. Without the slightest concern for pre-senting his own conduct in a somewhat more favorable light, he relates an occurrence that does him little honor, and he does so in what might be called the tone of a researcher, with soul-less indifference, as if he had every intention of defying his putative readers.

He relates that one day, shortly after unlocking his office, he came face to face with Luisito Rosales in the antechamber. Rosales, on the point of entering the president's office, was lead-ing a dog on a leash. "In a case like that," the private secretary remarks, "I would have been remiss in my duties as a private secretary if I had permitted him to do it, however much of a member of the cabinet he might be. 'But my dear Doctor,' I said to him, 'what are you thinking of? I can't let you appear in the presence of the Chief with that animal at your heels. Don't even think of it, Doctor, don't even think of it.' He stared at me crestfallen, searching my face for some sign that I might change my mind. I only confirmed my attitude: 'It's unthinkable,' and I added: 'Besides, you're not going to be able to see him this morning, with or without dog.' The old fool suddenly had irritated me, and I was not in the mood to let him in. He kept smiling at me, conciliating and propitiatory. He had made up his mind to share his secret with me (for ob-viously he had a secret connected with the dog) and to win me over to his side. He came up to me and said to me in a low voice, rolling his eyes like an accomplice, though there was no one else in my office: 'My dear Tadeo, this dog that you see here is a wonder, and will delight His Excellency. You can't imagine the surprise I'm bringing our great man. But you're going to taste the first fruits. Yes, you're going to have that privilege. Wait.' He looked all around him. 'Where can we go so that you can see in private what this little creature has learned to do?'

"I confess that the old man's manner had succeeded in whet-ting my curiosity. And as I had nothing better to do at the moment, I ordered the doorman not to let anyone in until further notice and went to lock myself into that very presidential bathroom where I had met the *caudillo* and his staff for the first time. The doctor and the dog went with me.

"'All right, let's see this nine-day wonder,' I said, crossing my arms when we were inside. I stood waiting. The doctor's only reply was to lift the little dog and set it down on the small side table next to the toilet and to take off its collar and leash. Immediately afterward, he planted himself in front of it, and with an abrupt movement, raised both his arms. The little beast, tense, on the alert, then began to open and close its mouth nervously. Don Luisito quickly hid his left hand behind his back while keeping his right in the air, then he made with it the signal the dog was waiting for. A feeble bark could be heard, followed by another, and another, and another, in time to the doctor's hand, which was beating out the rhythm: a slow, solemn and measured rhythm, later followed by a series of short, lively, martial barks. Finally I realized with astonishment that there could be no doubt about it—that dog was singing, if it may be called that, or barking. In short, he was performing our national anthem—he was performing it, and if the truth be known, rather well! An incredible feat. When the doctor had completed the second tempo, he let his hand fall and stood gazing at me. 'How's that?' his eyes were asking me with supreme satisfaction. I did not say a word; an idea was coming to me. I meditated a few moments, then asked him: 'Is this the surprise, then, that you're planning to offer the Chief for his birthday?"

"I saw from his face that I had hit the mark; my idea was working. The president's birthday was four days off, the occasion for great festivities, and the doctor hastened to declare with a gleam of enthusiasm in his eyes: 'Yes, precisely. That's it; that's it. But I wanted you to see it first, to work things out with you, to program it all so that the presentation would be a complete success. I think of the Polytechnic School ceremony for example; or perhaps here, or maybe . . .'

"He was very much excited; he had swallowed the bait. I

cut him short: 'So that's your plan. See here, Doctor, you're to leave the little dog with me until afternoon. Late in the day, either I'll bring it back to you or you can come to get it, whichever you prefer. I have to think. This is a serious business.'

" 'Leave the dog with you? Certainly not. Why do you want me to leave it? I'm never separated from this little fellow. You must understand that I feed him personally, and I don't let anyone else take care of him, only María Elena, my own daughter, whom I leave him with when I have to go out. I don't even trust Angelo, one of my own children, for everyone knows what boys are.'

"That made me angry. The old man had no faith in me. 'But come, come, Doctor, you're insulting me. That's a fine thing. So you come to me asking for help, and you won't even trust me!'

" 'Stop that, my boy. You don't have to be so sensitive. There's no need for you to fly into such a rage. In the first place, I have not said I don't trust you, only that I don't trust my own son.'

" 'And are comparing me now with such a . . . with Angelo? Come, Doctor, I beg of you.'

"He tried to protest his sincerity, but I wouldn't let him. 'Now, now,' I said peremptorily, putting the collar and leash on the little creature. 'You go along home, Doctor, and leave this clever fellow in my care, for I'm going to be busy arranging things in the way most suitable to you.'

"In short, I sent him off in a hurry. He was still protesting as he went down the stairs, offering me foolish advice. 'You may be sure I'll return for him this afternoon.'

"When I was alone, I could not decide yet what I would do with the dog. I went back to the bathroom where I had left him, looked at him, and said: 'So you're a clever dog, are you? Well, you're going to give me a private audition of the national anthem this minute.' And I planted myself in front of the little table, leash and all. I was laughing as I pictured myself imitating the doctor with both arms raised. 'Now!' I shouted at the dog and made the gesture with my hand, just as I had seen the old man do. But all to no avail! The sly little beast stared at me fixedly, never opening its mouth or showing any sign of feeling inclined to sing the melody. I repeated the mummery two or three times with no more effect. That infuriated me. I yanked him off the table. 'So Your Lordship will not deign to sing for this little black fellow, eh? Well, you just wait, wise dog!' I went out, looked in the drawer of my desk for a belt, and slowly made a slip knot in it with great care. Then I went back, passed the knot around the dog's neck and hanged him from a hook in the wardrobe. 'Now you can see who I am. I offer you my respects, Señor Caruso!' And I bowed as he was kicking in his last convulsions.

"When the doctor came back, quite early in the afternoon, I did not know what to say to him. 'Where's the dog?' he asked me immediately with suffocating anxiety. 'Sit down, Doctor, sit down right now.' He did so, with a smile that simulated complete confidence in me. But at the same time he was trying to read my tight, sober face from the corner of his eye. He began to chatter, and his loquacity seemed unquenchable. He told me how he had succeeded, by dint of patience, rewards, and punishments, in teaching that dog to modulate the anthem. He told me how the idea had happened to occur to him. His first glimmering, still vague and half-conscious must have come to him when, some time earlier, he had read in *Selecciones del Reader's Digest* about the fine accomplishment of a Brazilian bird breeder and patriot who had taught various kinds of birds to execute the national anthem in chorus by means of a clever, ingenious, and patient orchestration. That odd news item had aroused the doctor's enthusiasm, for he saw in it a demonstration of how man can conquer nature, the very songbirds of the forest, tame them into domesticity, by making them join their marvelous voices to sing the grandeur of their fatherland. One could picture the Brazilian standing in front of the cages, bringing in the several vocal parts under his baton.

" 'But actually, though that may have had some influence on me, what really awakened my inspiration was . . . you'd never guess what. Do you remember that day, during the parade, when a dog disrupted the solemnity of the performance with its furious barking and I went down from the presidential platform to give it a kick? It was then that a light dawned in my mind. The dog was barking in time; it was already tired, and I came up to give him the kick he deserved just as the band playing the anthem was seguéing from the *andante maestoso* to the *allegro,* and he began to change the rhythm, too, as he was barking. I said to myself then, Gosh! Well, that's how humanity's great inventions are born. All I had to do then was to find a docile little creature, intelligent, and with a good pitch, and to keep my patience with him to the end. I did that, and you have seen the fruits of it.'

"He interrupted himself to say: 'All right, come on, give me back my dog. I'm in a hurry. Have you thought about how we're going to present him to the Chief? You know now that I trust you. I'll not try to conceal from you that I am pinning my greatest hopes on that little creature to which I have devoted so much time. I am hoping for nothing short of my own moral retrieval through him. No more than that, but no less either. I'm not aspiring to win prizes, payment, or gifts; but I do want to present the Chief with an unmistakable manifestation of my pedagogical endowments so as to give the lie to the slanders of my enemies and opponents, who have been doing their best to discredit my work and impugn my competence as Minister of Public Instruction. No polemics in the newspapers, no arguments or rebuttals, just facts, facts! This modest little dog, which has been trained to sing the national anthem in front of His Excellency, and all by virtue of whom? Why thanks to the wit and the work of your humble servant, this so maligned and denigrated educator, Dr. Rosales in person, who, according to the prattling of those fools, hasn't a glimmering of what teaching is.'

"He burst out laughing at his nonsense. They would see now . . . Again he insisted that I return his dog to him. 'Come, where is my procurator? Where's that fellow who is less irrational than the people who are fighting me?'

"The old man was excited, euphoric, and that made me furious. 'Here, Doctor, come this way,' I said to him coldly, and I got up and walked toward the wardrobe. I opened the door and turned on the light.

" 'Where is he? I don't see him.' How could he see him if he looked at the floor? I pointed toward the object, which might have been taken for a handbag hanging from the hook. The doctor did not say a word, but his eyeglasses fell off him onto the floor. He picked them up. I took him by the arm and made him sit down in an armchair next to my big desk chair. He was pale and he kept eying me strangely.

"Then I took the floor and explained my reasons to him. In a slow, serious, firm voice I told him, mingling a tone of sorrowful reproach with one of affectionate protectiveness; 'It seems incredible, Doctor, that a man of your years and experience would run the risk. See here, I promised you I'd do the best I could for you, but *that* . . .'—I pointed to the door of the wardrobe —'. . . that, Doctor, was the best thing I could do for you, to eliminate the *corpus delicti*.' I paused a moment. 'Do you realize,' I went on, 'the irreverence signified by putting the national anthem into the mouth of a dog? Irreverence is the least of it. Indeed, it is a question of a crime, of treason to the fatherland. Just that. And yet, to suggest in addition such a mockery as that in the presence of the chief of state! But, Doctor, you're out of your mind . . . !'

"As I was speaking, I was observing the effect of my argument on him. The little man was annihilated. He kept staring at me, glassy-eyed, trying to understand, but he could not get over his shock. I went on, saying, 'Such folly! Who knows but that you might have been the one who had to hang himself in despair over the results of your unpremeditated and frivolous proposal, in place of that poor creature?' (I could feel myself talking as he himself was wont to talk; not in vain had he been my preceptor, for on serious occasions, I would adopt his style of delivery without meaning to.) 'For,' I continued, 'as a good friend to you, I am convinced that it was no more than a failure to reflect, not an intention to ridicule, that led you, a minister of the government, no less, to commit such a punishable act. You may consider yourself very fortunate to have met me by accident. Can you imagine the headlines in the *Army and National Police Bulletin,* the comments that López would make over the radio? But you may rest easy, Doctor, for you did have the good luck to meet me. Tell me, does anyone besides me know anything about this matter?'

"He shook his head slowly and sadly in negation as he licked my face with a doggy glance. The old busybody must have felt quite lost. My work was done; the subject was closed. But I went on expanding on the theme, to frighten and calm the little fellow by turns, and I even managed to make him thank me—with a handshake and the expression of his face, for he seemed to have lost the power of speech. Finally, when he was preparing to leave, I gave him a pat on the shoulder and drew from him a mournful smile. Then, with a few joking words, I concluded: 'Cheer up, Doctor. The timely death of that cur has saved you from the hangman. Treason to your country is a capital offense.' And, as usual, I ran my finger around my throat."

CHAPTER

17

✦✦✦✦✦✦✦✦✦✦✦✦✦✦✦✦✦✦✦✦✦✦✦✦✦✦✦✦✦

How dated, how distant, how trivial, how absurd in all their insignificance those stories seem now in view of what is happening all around me! I retreat from the world and bury my head in my papers so as not to think of the danger that lurks everywhere. But suddenly, when I am most distracted, I am carried away by a wretched vertigo, and I feel a kind of dizziness and nausea; everything around me begins to spin and it is as if I had awakened, unprepared, to the raw reality. "Can it be possible," I ask myself then, "can it be possible, Little Pinedo, that you are concerning yourself with, and at times even waxing indignant over, such nonsense? What importance can there be nowadays in the petty cruelty of a Tadeo Requena as he amuses himself by further unhinging the wretched Luisito Rosales with his oft-repeated, stupid joke about strangulation? Both of them are dead now, and strangulation and beatings and shootings and every other kind of horror are the order of the day, as if even the last shred of human feeling had vanished. The quarrels of yesterday strike us as sheer pettiness by comparison, for what is happening now has altered the rules of the past, has completely transformed the criteria formerly held valid." So it is that many people who used to detest Doña Concha, the president's wife, have come to pity her dreadful fate in the end, and they can even find some posthumous virtues in her. Alongside the laughable travesty calling itself a government which now has usurped the power, Antón Bocanegra's government seems worthy to be considered equal to that of Marcus Aurelius—so relative are the things of this life.

I myself—for I do not exclude myself—have had to modify some of my earlier judgments, and I feel no embarrassment in acknowledging that when I re-established contact with my Aunt Loreto in the midst of this mob scene, the difficulties and pressure of the circumstances weighing us all down made our conversation not only intimate and trusting, but even quite affectionate. On my side a sincere esteem was born for that poor woman whom explicable family reasons always had made me look upon with prejudice.

Old Olóriz, her kinsman, was the man who gave me her current address, and I had the pleasure of presenting myself to her, not in search of protection, for I no longer needed her for that, but rather in the attitude of one who might be able to offer protection to her. Indeed, when the tragic events that have brought us to this pass took place, growing out of the assassination of Bocanegra, and the *junta* of men whom in my mind I call the Three Trained Orangutans of Old Olóriz (naturally I never let that nickname pass my lips then, for this is no time for joking) had been installed in power, I considered the course of prudence to lie in cleaving to the old man and calling him my chief, in view of the fact that I always had done some actual work for the Special and Reserve Services, which he more or less controls. Doddering and wicked as he is, he also now controls the incredible trio that has climbed to the top and is presiding (let us put it that way, for they occupy the post of president and share it by thirds) over the destinies of the country, if you please, at this very moment.

Yes, his trained orangutans. They would have to be seen to be believed. What characters! What kittle-kattle! Ever since they made their first appearance on television—dark, with a most lugubrious look beneath the visors of their military caps pulled down to their eyebrows—I have had the sharp impression that the three sergeants of the revolutionary *junta* are nothing more than anthropoids escaped from a circus, and that they managed to clamber into the government only by surprise, only by a series of shocking coincidences. When television presented to the public the recently constituted Provisional Revolutionary Junta, we were in the Aurora Café, on the alert for news. Everyone seemed turned to ice, and no one permitted himself any comment whatsoever—no one except the inescapable Camarasa, of course, who made one of his macabre jokes. A most discreet silence! The humming of the ventilators was the only sound that could be heard when the images that had made such a deep impression on us faded from the screen. Who could those people be?

The background of that sinister lot became known before long, however. It turned out that the three of them had not suddenly surged up from anonymity to publicity, as had been believed. Though they were just beginning their novitiate in the field of politics, one of them at least, the one called Rufino Gorostiza, already had made his appearance in the newspapers. This man had enjoyed some earlier notoriety in the arena of free-for-all or catch-as-catch-can fighting, under the pseudonym of the Beast. Many fans immediately recalled with pleasure his famous bouts with Antonio Rodríguez (Superman), and they took particular pleasure in evoking the memorable knockout blow that he had landed on Gardenia the Beautiful, until then unbeatable. Those had been other times; all that belonged to the past. The Beast later took up the career of arms, where he quickly attained the rank of sergeant, and finally the dignity of the triumvirate, which he now shares with his colleagues, Falo Alberto of the mounted police and Tacho Castellanos, alias Salmagundi, from the Quartermaster Corps, who was conscripted into the offices of the presidential mansion when duty called him there, as everyone knows—owing to the situation that everyone also knows—to become a member of and to head the revolutionary *junta,* which was to rescue the fatherland alike from anarchy and from the threat of reaction ("the hydra of reaction" is the expression now in vogue). But what everyone did not know at the time, and many cannot imagine even yet, is that the real brain behind that group, the man who is pulling the strings, weaving the plots from inside his house, in short the master whose voice the Three Orangutans react to, is Old Olóriz, my dearly beloved administrator of the Special and Reserve Services.

I could not take my oath that it was he who was weaving the fabric of this government during those terrible hours of indescribable disorder and panic. I shall have to clear up that point some day. But in any case there can be no doubt that when these anthropoids discovered that they were on top, they ran docilely to feed on his wise and venerable advice. They, whom all the world distrusted, trusted him. I do not know how that valetudinarian managed to enslave their wills to such a point that he had them in his pocket. I do know, however, by a curious chance, that he was acquainted with the three and had had something to do with each of them—not only with Tacho Salmagundi, whose savings from the Quartermaster Corps had been handled very prudently by the old man, but with the Beast, too, back in his sporting days, and also with the other, the sergeant of police. So that when I visited and began to frequent the Olóriz house during the confusion of those first days, I never realized to what extent I was striking the right key. Mature reflection advised, of course, that I ought to shun contact with Doña Loreto, who had been living in the palace as the widow of a general of the old school and who belonged to the inner circle of the fallen regime, but instinct alone advised me as to which tree I should sit under in search of shade. I am living beneath his shelter, though no one could feel entirely safe at the side of this crafty old man. The very way in which he exercises his tremendous influence, without anyone's realizing it, without its being known, without a single one of the perquisites, advantages, or satisfactions of command apart from the fact of exercising it, permits me to remain near him, to see him at any hour of the day or night, to talk with him; but at the same time, it places me completely at his bidding, as if I were just another of the puppets that he manipulates with one finger and can drop whenever he desires and leave cast aside.

For all that, we still are alive, we are making shift with living. And during the past few days, it has seemed to me that it would be not imprudent now, perhaps the contrary, to seek out Loreto and obtain from her lips, while behaving as if I did not want to, the facts, valuable no doubt, that she and no one else possesses with regard to the genesis of the present events, which I am preparing to sketch. I am persuaded that the data that had been passed along to her as the friend, confidante, and perhaps accomplice of the First Lady not only would complement the information contained in the memoirs of the private secretary to the president, but also would serve to confirm or correct this information and would contain unsuspected elements, especially from the moment when Colonel Pancho Cortina put a period at the end of Tadeo Requena's scribblings. My hopes were not thwarted. Olóriz gave me the current address of Aunt Loreto, and after making an engagement with her by telephone, I went to visit her.

She was not in hiding, nor, unknowing as she was, did she believe that she could have any reason to go into hiding. When a band of outlaws had entered the palace and, under the pretext of looking out for the personal safety of the First Lady, had taken the former president's wife prisoner—an act that occurred on the day following Bocanegra's death—she, Loreto, simply had thrown the most necessary of her things hurriedly into a suitcase and had gone to seek hospitality at the door of a couple who were friends of hers. Several days later, Loreto's friends had fled to seek asylum on the other side of the frontier in a Dutch factory in which they owned some shares, and had left their entire house in her care to use as her own, as if it was nothing to lend her a roof over her head. There she was, settled in like a queen, when I came to see her.

It must be understood that our conversation turned out to be somewhat agitated in the beginning, a compound of excessive interest in our respective fortunes and of extravagant offers. I kept asking myself what that simpleton could be thinking of me, and I suppose that she, for her part, was asking herself something of the same sort about me: why the hell should I remember her and suddenly come looking for her? But after a short time we began to feel more comfortable with each other, and the conversation finally stretched out over several hours. How many horrors had been required to melt the ice between us, after years and years.

I started off by asking her how she had weathered the storm, and it was then that she told me of Doña Concha's arrest and all the incidents that followed it. It had taken her more than a week to find out where her friend was, and after learning that she was a prisoner in the ancient asylum of the Immaculate Conception, she had had to spend many more days in obtaining a permit to see her—only to find her dead! For when they finally let her into the infirmary, after additional postponements, she had to confront that horrible spectacle. Of course Loreto hastened to claim the body so that her friend could be decently buried, and at the same time moved heaven and earth with her demand that the crime should not go unpunished. In point of fact, and granting that when the dog is dead he's cured of the rabies, as the saying goes, they had got themselves out of the mire by performing with dispatch that business of the pistol shot into the one who would seem to have committed the murder, an idiot from the asylum who had wandered around like a lost soul after being "liberated" by the revolution, always pilfering with the pitying permissiveness of the former *concièrge* and then warden of the prison. This good man, very dutiful in his own judgment, was the one who acquainted Loreto with everything that had happened since Doña Concha had been installed in the Immaculate Conception.

"But there are things . . ." he would frequently interrupt himself to say. "You must forgive me, *señora*, but such things are unsuitable for a lady's ears." Then she would have to comfort him by saying again and again that she had been like a sister to the prisoner and that she wished, indeed absolutely needed, to be brought up to date about everything. In the end she was apprised of the ignominies to which the illustrious prisoner had been obliged to lend herself, in greater or smaller degree. Loreto was of the opinion that the lady's mind surely must have been addled by so many disasters. Otherwise, how could her conduct reach such extremes of folly, such . . .

As the saying goes, I should have liked to stick my finger down her throat and make her throw it all up. Accordingly I interrupted her at this point: "But, forgive me, I don't know how to put it, but in that terrain, she never . . . in short, no one was unaware . . ." I even slipped in an allusion to the affair with Tadeo.

Seeing that I already knew (and this tactic, repeated each time she tried to hold back something from me, infallibly brought results), she set aside her reservations and answered that yes, it was true, but she felt sure, nonetheless, that the poor thing must have been forced to it in the beginning because, granted that she was not fastidious, still she was nobody's fool, and what she had been doing in the prison amounted to something worse than foolishness.

"I don't know, I don't know," my aunt concluded, shaking her head. Her friend had turned out to be as incomprehensible to her in death as she had been in life. "She was quite mad," she said. "And I was swimming with the current and was still madder."

She had become depressed. Her eyes were lowered and her voice choked; she had reached the softening point. Like one also discreetly alluding to his own personal case, I let fall the observation that it is too painful to have to live in solitude and that one is always obliged to swim in someone else's current. Antenor's death must have been a blow to her. Groping, I had touched a sore spot. She grew very excited and began to confide to me the story of the marvelous Presence just as it appears earlier in extract, speaking with some hesitation and only after an infinite number of preambles. She confessed to me that from the very moment of the revelation, she had not spent a single moment without the hope, never yet realized, of finding her lost treasure again in some form, "of at least remembering the name, hearing his accents again," now that she could not see him. She finished with her hands clasped as if in prayer, her heavy, lustrous eyelids veiling her faded eyes. I was listening to her, and I did not know whether to be astonished at her eccentricity or to pity her for her feelings. In any case, the fact that, unless she was shocked or confused, the poor woman had had such a dream while her husband was dying of a heart attack beside her in the bed cannot fail to make an impression. And even on the supposition (which, of course, cannot be overlooked) that it was all a fantasy constructed *a posteriori,* her anxiety was no less real, her obsession no less painful, her mania no less pathetic.

"And you have never since had any hint, any new sign, anything at all?" I asked her.

"Nothing," she answered me emphatically. "Would you believe it, Pinedo? Nothing, literally nothing, I give you my word." And she stared at me in silence.

She went on to tell me that in order to help her, Doña Concha had insisted she should try her luck at the séances, where a group of distingushed persons, educated and serious, established a weekly contact with the Beyond from a little side parlor in the palace, on the First Lady's initiative. Loreto had taken her place there to please her friend—she could not possibly have refused her—and had begun to apply to the spirits, "but with little hope, as you can imagine. For how was I to invoke him if the difficulty lay in the very fact that I could not manage to recall his name? To call him by Antenor's would have been a cry in the wilderness. It would even have seemed like a mockery after the revelation he had made to me of his real personality, so unlike . . . without depreciating Antenor, it was most unlike his—if you will forgive me for saying so. How can I put it? Antenor was a very good man; he never did any harm to anyone, and he was considerate even in dying. He did it without a struggle, without causing any trouble, except for the inevitable shock, of course. But in any case, how can I compare them? I wish you could understand."

I understood. "So then never? . . ."

"Never. Except that one time some mischievous spirit, some mocker or some fool (for naturally there are that kind, too) tried to play a joke on me by addressing me and attempting to pass himself off as the marvelous Presence. He came to me and said: 'Do you recognize me, Loreto?' As if we were at a masquerade. 'Look here, Loreto; I am that man whom you know.' But when I pressed him and ordered him to pronounce his name, the wretch tried to go off at a tangent. 'You know me very well,' he replied. 'I'm the Sacred Heart of Jesus.' I told him to go fly a kite with his rotten jokes. But what wouldn't I have given, what wouldn't I give, to feel that he was speaking to me again?"

I soothed her mind as best I could. But at the same time I seized the opportunity to venture the opinion that dealings with spirits always turn out to be chancy and may lead to very serious consequences, and that many of the evils that have rained down on our heads and still are pouring over them were stirred up in those very Tuesday séances, where, on the other hand, she had not caught the faintest glimmer of light. Say that a mocking spirit had tried to play a cruel joke; if so, other, malevolent spirits had deceived young Requena, had exploited his ambitions and persuaded him into doing what was to ruin him and the entire country.

Loreto meditated a moment, then smiled. At times she does not seem so stupid. "The spirits are not to blame for everything," she said finally. "Or at any rate they are not the most to blame in this case." She was recognizing that in reality her friend Doña Concha had been the one to take the decisive steps there, with great terror on her part, but without having it in her to avert anything. By the time she realized what she was doing, things already had been done, or half-done, and there was no possibility of turning back. "The truth is," she mused, "that Concha was a kind of tornado. She dragged us all along until she herself collapsed and was swallowed up in the vortex of her own paroxysms."

CHAPTER

18

✦✦✦✦✦✦✦✦✦✦✦✦✦✦✦✦✦✦✦✦✦✦✦✦✦

This conversation with my Aunt Loreto, which lasted several hours, has enabled me to learn, among many other things of positive interest, some invaluable details surrounding the death of Bocanegra, the particulars of which had appeared destined to remain as hidden as those concerning the murder of a very remote Gothic king. Loreto informed me that on that terrible night, after she was asleep for no one knows how long, her friend came at some time around dawn to arouse her by knocking urgently on the door of her room, and then burst in upon her like a waterspout, with hair disheveled, and threw herself face down on the bed without a word. Not until after a very long interval and many pleas did she announce briefly in a cold, apathetic voice, "Tadeo has killed Bocanegra." ("Even when she was talking to me," Loreto explained to me, "she used to call her husband Bocanegra, not Antón.") Then Concha added, "Out of jealousy!"

"You can imagine, Pinedo, how dumfounded that left me!

'Out of jealousy!' For the moment I was not thinking of the tremendous consequences of that piece of news; I was thinking, 'Out of jealousy!' and I could not believe it. It's not impossible that a lover may feel jealous of the husband, not even very un-usual. But Tadeo jealous? I knew all too well how stormy the intimate scenes between that odious boy and the mad Concha used to be; more than once the unpleasant role of witness and mediator had fallen to my lot. But it never was a question of jealousy. It was because he detested her and struggled against her with the desperation of a man carrying a stone around his neck, a stone that he is crazy to get rid of but cannot. He used to insult her, and one day in front of me he gave her a shove that made her stagger back into an armchair. 'Out of jealousy!' No, out of loathing, out of aversion. As for her, she had come to loathe him, too, from the bottom of her heart. If I were to tell you, Pinedo . . .

"But to go on: while all those things were going through my mind, she was still lying face down on my bed. Then bang! I heard a shot. Only one, quite plainly, and then silence again. Concha, whose head was still buried in her arms, reared up, sniffing the air like a dog. Then suddenly she sprang to her feet at one bound and said to me in a tense voice, but now almost gaily: 'Did you hear that? I'm going to find out what that's all about right now.' She picked up the extension telephone that we had had installed in my dressing room and tried to get in touch with Colonel Cortina. I was badly confused. I did not understand one thing. I thought that Tadeo must have killed himself after committing a crime like that. But Concha was yelling at Pancho Cortina and telling him to come at once, that something very serious had happened, that the president, knowing that he had been betrayed by that miserable Tadeo Requena, had just liqui-dated him. My head was spinning.

"'You know I'm not leaving my hiding place, Pancho, until the situation is cleared up,' she said in conclusion. 'Cleared up, do you understand?'"

"I was the one who did not understand, Pinedo. I assure you my head was reeling. During the first moments I believed, as I say, that the chances were that Tadeo had shot himself. That one report, in the silence of the night, could mean nothing else if what she had told me on entering my room was true. But now it was turning out that . . . Later it became known—the radios and periodicals were shouting it—that the shot had in fact been fired by the secretary, Tadeo Requena, who had assassinated his chief in the most treacherous fashion, and that he had even made use of Bocanegra's own pistol, as the latter lay in bed. What Concha had told me at the very beginning was true, then . . . At the moment when she told me, however, no shot whatever had been heard as yet. That is something I don't understand. If I am in my right mind, that couldn't be true; there's a mystery here, and however much I turn and twist it I cannot manage to unravel it."

I kept smiling to myself inwardly. Tadeo's frank memoirs already had handed me the key to the mystery; I had read in advance the dénouement of the plot unraveled in the final pages of the novel, and, like a detective who keeps certain clues up his sleeve so as to surprise the reader, I was in a position to solve the puzzle. Here was the First Lady accusing her lover, Secretary Requena, of having killed the chief of state, her husband, and yet the lethal shot was not heard until later. A problem! But I felt no desire at all to offer the solution to Loreto. I asked another question: "Just how do you explain that no one responded to the sound?"

"That is what I kept asking myself during those moments, for I could see that actually no one had made a move. But, after all, that isn't so strange. To begin with, most of the employees sleep outside the palace, and those who did spend the night there or who used to sleep there were in another wing, while our rooms lay alongside the offices. Besides, if anyone were to hear a shot coming from our part, he would conclude that the best thing to do was to pull the covers up over his head and lie frozen so as to avoid any involvements. As for the bodyguards, they stayed some distance away. The result is that it was not until the later series of shots—one, two, three, four—fired to execute the magnacide most summarily by Pancho Cortina's own hand, which was followed immediately by Cortina's fall down the stairs, did people start to reach the scene. As for Cortina's behavior, doesn't it seem to you, Pinedo, that it had been rather odd and daring? He comes, accompanied by not more than three or four men, and even leaves them at the foot of the stairs. He goes up alone to confront who knows what kind of situation. And then, instead of arresting the secretary, he kills him on the spot. How can anyone understand that?"

"Doesn't it seem to you, Aunt Loreto, that if it wasn't jealousy that motivated Tadeo, it might very well have been fear?" I asked her. "Fear that Bocanegra might have been told, I mean . . ."

"Bocanegra didn't know a thing," she replied. "Nor did he want to know a thing. Toward the end, the only thing that Bocanegra was interested in was the bottom of the glass. And other bottoms," she added with an enigmatic smile.

I could not manage to get another word out of her concerning this insinuation. Naturally, I think that she was not referring to ship's bottoms in mentioning those "other bottoms." I may succeed at some propitious moment during another interview with her in finding out about the intimate affairs of the palace, which she knows better than anyone. Why shouldn't she pass them on to me? With all that water over the dam, with things the way they are, what can it matter to her now? It matters to me as a historian; the historian must rise above the waters. And in that sense, I cannot complain of the results of that visit; the data she delivered into my hands were of the first magnitude. I was not going to be led off into bypaths, either. I wanted to know in concrete detail what had been the actual intentions and actions of the betrayers in the drama, together with their relationships, and particularly what had to do with her, for I already had his confession, made in advance—an almost daily confession—in the smudged pages of his prolix manuscript.

"Hasn't it occurred to you, Aunt Loreto, that Tadeo may have done what he did at the instigation of Doña Concha?" I asked, hoping to prime her to talk.

"See here, Pinedo, the matter is not that simple. I don't know and I wouldn't dare say yes or no. The final events are not all that clear to me."

"But it wouldn't be so very strange if she was full of resentment; if, as you say, she saw that Bocanegra, who no longer interested her, was interested, on the other hand, in those mysterious bottoms, or little bottoms that you haven't cared to explain to me about."

"All right!" she said, wavering. "There was no lack of reasons for her to feel so. Who could ever understand Bocanegra? People who keep so quiet frighten one after a while. To think that Concha had been everything to that man during those wild years of their struggle, when they hadn't a bite to put in their mouths! Antón Bocanegra would never have crawled out of the ditch if it hadn't been for her help! You see, Pinedo, he was a walking failure; he was carrying his failure inside him like a cancer, and it was evident later that his rise to power did not signify regeneration, but rather a broadening and deepening of his vocation for failure, so that everyone has had a share in it, and we have all been sunk by it."

I was struck dumb at hearing those words from Loreto's lips. What on earth? Could it be she who was talking like that? No, it was not she. She became aware of how I was eying her, of my surprise, and she reddened a little beneath her powder base and makeup, and declared: "A gentleman who is a friend of mine, the owner of this house where we're sitting now, in fact, had known Bocanegra since their student days at the university and he used to explain it all to me."

I smiled then and could not keep from making a little joke. "Ah!" I cried, "I was thinking that the marvelous Presence must have breathed that sentence into your ear."

I should never have said that. It brought back to her mind the subject of the marvelous Presence, which so obsessed her, and I had a hard job bringing her around to our subject again.

That taught me a lesson about not interrupting her in the future, though to be sure I had to bite my tongue more than once. But I let her speak whatever nonsense came into her head, and it was better so, for in that way I could cast over the movement captained by Antón Bocanegra the kind of retrospective glance that is so conducive to the objectivity of the historian. If I had ventured to contradict her, she would have drawn back into her shell like a snail. All the while she was keeping me on tenterhooks the good woman was abandoning herself to the bittersweet pleasures of memory, and her divagations sketched for me the portrait of a young Bocanegra—full of fire, of generosity, of love for the disinherited of the earth (his inveterate plebeianism had become love for the poor; his irresponsible verbalizing, generosity; his disgruntled rancor, ardor; and the shameless demagoguery of the Father of the Poor, his talent)—whom that self-sacrificing woman had aided, comforted, and followed, abandoning everything to his work of redemption at the cost of her own interests and every other consideration. Had they actually seen themselves like that? In such idyllic colors and outlines? Loreto kept harping on the importance of the role played by her friend Concha, stressing her virtues, and finding excuses for her arrogance and follies in her hour of triumph by citing her fears, anxieties, fatigues, poverty, and worries during the "heroic" period.

At this point I thought it opportune to slip in a provocative little question. "I know," I granted, slightly sardonic beneath my mask of sincerity, "that Bocanegra could not have done all he did without her. But tell me, Loreto, don't you think that even though she may have been useful to him in the beginning, she did him an equal amount of harm in the end?"

"Let me tell you," was her reply, "that my departed Antenor . . ." (the marvelous Presence again? No, this time it was Antenor Malagarriga himself) ". . . my departed Antenor used to prophesy that that lady's meddling would cause the president serious trouble someday. But you know as well as I do that toward the end your dear uncle was constantly afraid the government might turn against him; and even on the day of our silver wedding anniversary, the day of his death, too, he was going around repeating with considerable rancor that he was fed up and on the verge of saying to hell with everything. As for me, I can't deny that she did; but we must still give the devil his due. Bocanegra was stubborn, that gentleman, stubborn as a mule, and consequently he wouldn't truckle to his spouse as much as people think. He gave her her head and, sly fellow that he was, he laid the ground for her to be blamed for all the mistakes, but when he honestly did not want something, he dug in his heels right there, and no one on earth could move him."

A pause ensued. I was thinking the obvious: that ultimately mere opposition is good for nothing but to curb the grossest barbarities, but that in operating a government the important factor is always the initiative. And it would seem that basically Bocanegra was very slack-willed, perhaps because his will worked best in destroying whereas it was generally lax in the face of actual work. Without mentioning this appraisal of mine, I phrased my thoughts for Loreto: the president did sometimes pull in his horns, but she always sang the leading voice. Of course I had no intention of arguing such questions with my interlocutress. I preferred rather to extract facts from her, and I added: "If she wasn't like that, give me one single example of an important decision adopted against her will."

I succeeded in getting one that was beyond my expectations.

"Against her will? Well, the appointment of Rosales as Minister of Instruction, to go no further," she told me.

My eyes opened as round as saucers. I showed that I was greatly surprised, and my astonishment flattered Loreto. "It can't be possible," I said. "Wasn't she the one who . . . after all, hadn't it been her idea to bring respectable people into the government— people like my uncle Antenor?"

"You'll see. The case of Antenor was quite different. To begin with, neither Antenor nor any one of you had put up the unrelenting opposition that was raised by the Rosales from their estate in San Cosme. My husband, good rest to him, was a meek and gentle dove, and I always tried to keep him away from evil influences. Besides, you must understand that my friendship with the president's wife was bound to be of some use. On the other hand, Concha had always seen it as why invite the enemy into the house by making Rosales a minister? She would gladly have exterminated the whole lot. I grant you that she was implacable in this instance. And how she fought with Bocanegra to try to prevent what, in the last analysis, she could not! I remember that she went so far as to insult him, after exhausting all her arguments, even the argument that an appointment like that was tantamount to acknowledging that they were responsible for the death of the senator and were offering the family a kind of bashful guilt compensation. When he finally signed the appointment and she saw that she had not had her own way, she let more than two weeks go by without addressing a word to her husband. I think it was from that moment that she began to feel alienated from him, and that everything started at that point."

"But why such a rage? Why all that African hatred for the unfortunate Luisito? After all, wasn't the aggressive member of the Rosales family dead already?"

She smiled, and only then did I realize the malicious meaning that might be attributed to my remark as I recalled the episode of the mutilation, and I felt annoyed with myself for using the word "member" in that particular context. As a matter of fact, it turned out to be a lucky blunder, for Loreto, doubtless suspecting that I knew much more about the matter than I seemed to, made up her mind after a moment's hesitation to talk to me with some frankness.

"You must understand," she told me, "that a woman can never forgive certain kinds of offenses. And that animal of a Lucas Rosales had treated Concha as a common prostitute."

Upon hearing that, I had hard work to restrain the irony that was on the tip of my tongue. I wanted to say, "Common is hardly the word for it," but it was to my advantage to let her talk and explain herself, to let her think that I was in the know and to avoid putting my foot into it at the wrong time.

My discretion bore rich fruit. I had been a long way from suspecting that the whole dirty business carried out by Chino López had been nothing but the vengeance of a woman scorned. I was far from suspecting that during the *prehistoric* days, the woman who in due course was to be the First Lady of the Republic had had anything to do with the proud, grand gentleman, or that ultimately he could be blamed for nothing but having helped her to reach the place where she was. Doubtless that scheming woman had tested her weight on various ladders before tying her fortunes to those of the lubberly Bocanegra. I had not known either that it was in San Cosme that she had met Bocanegra, during a period when he was staying there, long before he had given any thought to politics. At the time he was dedicating himself wholeheartedly to one of those ridiculous business ventures which he expected to yield enormous profits, a chimera that inevitably had dissolved in his hands, leaving him no solace but rum. At that time, she had gone to San Cosme and was a guest in the only hotel in the village, above the grocery store owned by the Galician, Luna. Her intention was to pursue Don Lucas Rosales and, if necessary, to involve him in a scandal in full view of his family. The budding friendship established later with Bocanegra dissuaded her and deflected her plans. And no sooner had the business venture of the hawthorns—the speculation in question—proved illusory than they both vanished from the town in search of better luck.

What times those were! He was to continue to dream up new and fascinating ventures, and to talk about them, and to plan them, and to get entangled in them up to his eyes, and to fail several more times before he was to discover his political vocation out of his pity for the poor, suffering people and himself.

"How true it is," Loreto observed, "that without that woman —Concha—Bocanegra never would have done what he did, nor he have arrived where he did arrive! He was not without talent; you could see that then. But it was she, she and no one else, who not only gave him the idea (the idea itself is nothing), but also added the drive, the staying power, the courage, the indomitable will that a crusade of such a nature calls for, especially in the beginning, when one is a nobody and any claim seems overly daring."

She rose from her chair and went to rummage in a desk drawer. Then she handed me a yellowing photograph. There was Bocanegra, wearing his leggings and with a broad-brimmed hat down over his eyes, surrounded by his general staff drawn from the "Penniless Poor." And among them, the only woman in the group, was Doña Concha, smiling into the camera, still very young in appearance, seeming almost a girl. What was she showing me that for? I had a strange feeling, a kind of nausea or vertigo, I don't know what.

"This is a document in itself, an item for an historical museum," I said as I handed it back to her.

What I was particularly interested in finding out were the details of the death of Senator Rosales, but either Loreto did not know them or did not want to pass them on. She did assure me that the assassination on the steps of the capitol had not been Doña Concha's doing, or, at any rate, that she had not arranged it. But Loreto's information did not go beyond that. What struck me was that the woman had not considered her accounts closed even when the offender had been liquidated. The president's wife had found it intolerable that Don Luisito, the other brother, later had entered the government—intolerable to the point at which she never could forgive her husband for it. Clearly the ancient and unmentionable affront by Rosales had by then been reclothed in the guise of political hatred, which provided ready grounds, seemingly impersonal or above personalities, for carrying on the grudge. Bocanegra's act in decreeing that appointment, which she had fought with such vehemence, seemed to her not merely a slap in the face, but something bordering on disloyalty to the cause for which they had fought side by side, and even a betrayal of the people.

"So that if things are traced back to their original sources, in the final analysis what cost Bocanegra his life must have been that decision of his to place one of the Rosales brothers in the cabinet," I summed up in a tone of conjecture. Loreto blinked, not fully understanding me at first. "I say," I explained, "granted that the first serious disagreement was determined by that, and that it constituted a cause for resentment to . . ."

"Yes, yes, that's it," she hastened to say. "Everything that happened could be considered a reprisal against the Rosales family. To a certain extent. A posthumous revenge. Would you like me to tell you something? In the bottom of her heart Concha still was afraid of them. She not only hated them; she was afraid of them, too. Strange as it may seem, once she had succeeded in toppling them from their power, her hatred was transformed into fear when she saw them destroyed. I am convinced that her attitude (quite irrational, as Bocanegra used to say with reproach), her blind opposition to the appointment of Don Luisito as Minister of Instruction, was more or less dictated by fear. What may be called irrational fear. Irrational, but as we were able to see later, quite justified."

I held my tongue and waited. I had begun to realize that strange thoughts were churning in her harebrained head, and I did not want to scatter them or deflect them by bringing home to her the fact that Doña Concha, out of resentment toward her husband, or ambition, or whatever it may have been, had been the very one to unleash the catastrophe. Instead of saying that, I confined myself to a soothing reflection: "The truth is," I said, "that one will ever know."

"Or if anyone ever does find out, there's no help for it now," she replied. What would be the point in quibbling over that? She went on: "For all her fear, she was nonetheless imprudent, the poor creature, and she could not keep quiet. She paid for it dearly! Fear paralyzes some people, but not her; she could not keep still."

She was staring at the ceiling, and I followed her gaze. The ceiling was painted cream color, with absurd garlands of flowers in the center and at the corners. She kept squirming in her wicker chair, and I noticed her feet, somewhat swollen in the shoes she had forced onto them in order to receive my call. She went on in a dreamy tone: "If one has things on his conscience, it's best to leave the dead in peace. And who doesn't have something on his conscience when he's no longer so young? In the end, Tadeo Requena himself was struggling like a cat on its back. As for me, let me tell you this—I never liked that little game of calling up the spirits. You stick a finger into the electric cables and, of course, you wind up getting the current through you. But whenever she took something into her head, there was no resisting her. A fine shock she got, too. She was shaken to her entrails when the spirit of Senator Rosales appeared like a clap of thunder in the middle of a rather dull séance! He broke in with his usual brusque manner, and I don't need to tell you it shook us all. The medium turned rigid as a stick and struck her head a tremendous blow against the wall. Then she began to talk in such a high-flown style that it alone would have been enough to make you recognize the senator speaking through her. He had come for the purpose of passing on a message to Tadeo; an order rather, for actually it was an order. Concha got upset; I had never seen her look so ashen, so terrified as at that moment."

As I kept listening to what Loreto had started to tell me, you may be sure I hardly dared to breathe. I was drinking in her

[135]

words, trembling to think that she might yet thwart me at any moment by repenting of the confidences she was bestowing on me, perhaps without calculating clearly just how far she was going.

I risked a little gambit, hoping to forestall that. "But . . ." I wondered. "Well now, couldn't that all have been a farce cooked up by Doña Concha so as to induce her lover? Pretending to be terrified? I don't say that . . ."

"Believe me, Pinedo," she answered, "as surely as my name is Loreto she was a long way from 'putting on.' Our friendship didn't start yesterday. I'd seen her in tight spots before, I can assure you. She might have been able to deceive someone else, but not me. The attack of nerves she suffered later in my room was no joke, and we were alone together. Nor were the cruel insults she heaped on the medium the next day, calling her a sow, as if the poor thing were to blame for the language used by Rosales. She even threatened her with the police and jail. Naturally she didn't do anything, for she knew perfectly well that the dead can laugh at cells and prisons. She did fire that medium, an excellent one who later redeemed herself. On the following Tuesday the senator appeared again to repeat and confirm through the lips of another person the charge he had laid upon Tadeo to free the country from tyranny unless he himself wanted to succumb at its hands. From that day until her horrible death, poor Concha did nothing but make mistakes, like a person acting under the pressure of terror."

"What about Tadeo?" I asked then. "What was his reaction? Could he have believed in the message?"

"The fact that he ended up by assassinating Bocanegra shows that he did believe it and that he obeyed it, even though he struggled at first. The boy was very stubborn, but he fell into the trap. I am under the impression that all he needed to make him give in was the evidence that the other Rosales, Don Luisito, whose passing was then quite recent (it couldn't have been more than a month since he had committed suicide), should come, as indeed he did come, to re-enforce the terrible warnings of the senator with his own persuasive words."

CHAPTER

19

++++++++++++++++++++++++++

Now that I have come this far, I realize that as yet I have not even mentioned the end that Don Luisito Rosales came to. He tendered a voluntary and irrevocable resignation of his position by quitting this life, as the Spanish Minister Plenipotentiary put it jokingly and in somewhat doubtful taste when writing one of his accomplished reports.

The truth is that these notes of mine are turning out to be too disorganized; it seems to me they are even chaotic, perhaps owing to the general disorder that surrounds one everywhere today or to the nervousness we all suffer from, plus the uncertainty in which one has to work. When I am able to edit the definitive text of my book with greater calm and under more normal circumstances, I shall have to be on the alert and take great care not to present events all jumbled together as they are now, but in their proper chronological order, so as to make them quite intelligible and thus to display the formal decorum demanded by an historical account. After all, this does not matter; these papers are nothing more than an exercise, like those played by musicians while tuning up their instruments or, at best, like a compilation of materials, a rough copy, and an annotation of details meant to keep me from forgetting later what occurs to me now and what I ought to retain. In any case, I am the only one who has to cope with them.

To go on, then. I shall follow the custom I have adopted and register the circumstances surrounding the suicide of Don Luisito, using as a basis such documents as I possess and referring for the nonce to the newspapers I have collected, which are to be kept here as a secondary source available to the historian.

Because of the dirty trick the poor man had played in taking leave of this indecent life, the press was short on information and strangely discreet in its commentaries on everything having to do with the death of the Minister of Public Instruction. The official prose of the Spanish diplomat is more explicit as to details. In addition, his writings offer the advantage of enabling us to trace an objective picture of the general situation as if against a backdrop. Although I am not in agreement with him on all points, I am keeping his script here as hard news, along with other documents I am fortunate enough to have at my disposal, so that they may serve to illustrate this short passage from our contemporary history.

The Spanish minister addresses his superiors in the following terms: "As I had the honor of informing Your Excellency through my telegram of yesterday, the Minister of Public Instruction, Dr. Luisito Rosales, resigned his position voluntarily and irrevocably on that same day by taking his own life at an early hour of the morning. The funeral ceremonies are over. I had to attend them after I had presented the government with my official condolences, and tonight I feel I am in duty bound to fill out the news item for Your Excellency with some complementary details.

"First of all, details concerning the personality of the deceased. As Your Excellency knows from earlier reports, and particularly because I had the honor to write you when Dr. Rosales was appointed to the cabinet with the portfolio of Public Instruction, the said gentleman belonged to one of the oldest families in the country, today dispossessed and almost sequestered by the political movement espoused by the present chief of state. Dr. Rosales was a brother of the famous Don Lucas Rosales, a landowner and politician, who, as Your Excellency may perhaps recall, aroused active opposition to the regime of Bocanegra and was shot down for that reason on the steps of the capitol. Only the peculiarities of these people, whose psychology, sociology, and public customs emerge in remarkable manifestations that are in every way incomprehensible to one not intimately integrated with their daily life, can explain the fact that in spite of everything, a brother of his could later bring himself to accept a somewhat prominent position of some responsibility within the said regime.

"Yet you may remember that President Bocanegra also belongs himself in some way (the way known as black sheep, outcast, bohemian) to the group of distinguished families who were once omnipotent in this country. Thus, you may begin to understand the case of Don Luis Rosales, however incongruous and scandalous may be the collaboration of a person endowed with certain qualities with a government that is not distinguished for its adherence to the norms of the most elementary decency, make whatever reservations you will. Dr. Rosales was unquestionably an educated man, cultivated and well-mannered, though, it must be admitted, somewhat eccentric. His habits and certain traits of his character had robbed him of the reputation that can be glimpsed only dimly here; it must even be recognized that he often earned to the fullest his name for picturesquesness. In addition, his attitude toward the Mother Country was exceptionally favorable. Everything Spanish won his esteem if not his enthusiasm by the mere fact of being Spanish, though on the other hand he suffered from an incomprehensible Francophilic weakness that might barely be excused as a hangover from his youthful studies in Paris. In spite of this last trait, his demise must be reckoned a real loss from our points of view.

"During my visit of condolence to the chancellor, I inquired discreetly into the reasons that might have driven his fellow cabinet member to the fatal resolution to cut short his days. He told me that the suicide had not left a letter, nor a will, nor an explanation of any kind, but that for some time serious fears had been increasingly entertained with regard to his mental state. Then he went on to tell me, laughing a good deal, several anecdotes already known to me.

"While the funeral obsequies (which took place after a brief wake in the offices of the Secretariat of Public Instruction, for the death had occurred in the mansion of the deceased, far from the capital, and the body had to be brought from a considerable distance, with all the inconveniences arising from a hot climate) —in the course of the funeral, that is, I had occasion to exchange impressions with the Argentine ambassador, Dr. Menotti, whose conjectures on the causes of the suicide cannot fail to be invested with some political interest. According to Menotti, Dr. Rosales must have put a wrong foot forward or been cheated in his dealings with Bocanegra. When he agreed to enter the service of the regime, thereby renouncing his brother's interests and any vindication of the senator's memory, he must have been hoping, perhaps had been expressly or tacitly promised, that the senator's property would pass into his hands by means of some judicial or administrative ploy, once the widow and the children had been expatriated, for after the senator's death, his conduct had been the object of investigative proceedings, and his fortune had been attached pending the settlement of any liens against it. In the end that property was definitively confiscated except for the family mansion (Dr. Rosales being granted its usufruct). Bocanegra no longer needed him then, and our man found himself holding cards no longer worth playing. At the same time he realized from various indications that they were preparing to dismiss him like a servant or even to sue him on some trumped-up charge, so that, with such a prospect before him, the wretch chose to hang himself.

"Incidentally, my Argentine colleague called to my attention that the obsequies for the Minister of Public Instruction were much less splendid than those for his brother, who had gone down fighting. That observation was quite correct. No mourning crowd like the earlier one was there, and conversely, the president did not deign to honor the funeral rites with his presence on the official side. Instead he delegated the task of delivering the funeral oration to his chancellor, who discharged it with a generous use of common platitudes.

"I must also add that before the mourners took leave of one another a rumor began to spread among the retinue to the effect that two days earlier a medical specialist had announced to poor Rosales a diagnosis of cancer of the liver. If this piece of news is true, it would go far to justify the suicide of the Minister of Public Instruction on psychological, if not moral, grounds.

"As for the foreseeable consequences, in my opinion no important innovations in the public order may be expected from the absence of Dr. Rosales, if we except the necessary filling of the vacant post. It would be difficult to put forth anything other than straight guesswork and gratuitous speculation with regard to that, given the limitless arbitrariness that marks President Bocanegra's appointments. We may expect that some waspish, opportunistic, and unscrupulous newspaperman will assume the portfolio, or else some obscure schoolmaster, but it is not beyond the bounds of possibility that some municipal secretary, some lawyer, or some labor leader may occupy the cabinet seat."

As we can see, the Spanish diplomat's report is complete, and shrewd in the bargain. What Tadeo Requena has left in his memoirs regarding his personal involvements in the emergency pretends—I say pretends—to be fully as unfeeling as this bureaucratic account. Tadeo goes to extremes here in the use of the detached, cynical tone, so much so that he leaves a contrary impression in the end, an impression that he is boasting and that his braggadocio is not merely rhetorical. But you may judge from his own words, which I shall confine myself to copying.

He starts off with a string of bad-tempered exclamations. "Of course," he protests with displeasure, "the honor of having to struggle with the problem had to fall on me! A dirty little errand! What glory for me to have to deal with the matter as His Excellency's personal representative! To begin with, a long trip, miles and miles of jolting over the roads, and all as if an undertaking like that were nothing. What was the old man thinking of? Why did he have to to San Cosme for that? As if there weren't hooks enough here in the capital for him to hang himself from! No, he had to do it from a big beam in his own house. And to have to go and hang himself after all! Couldn't he have told us good-bye in some other way, say a romantic pistol shot, the poison of the Borgias, opening his veins like his master Socrates [so he says: I am confining myself to transcribing], or throwing himself into the water or else through a window, or going on a hunger strike, or merely waiting a little while with a pinch of patience for his hour to come? For, after all, how much time could he have left to him? No! He had to choose to die like a dog, in that particular way. He did it only to annoy everyone else, of course. And here I am; I had never gone back to the village, and I'd been flattering myself with the prospects of treating myself to that pleasure some day, just like anyone else. I wanted to prepare a fine reception for myself in my home town. Then all of a sudden, go right this minute, ready or not, and hurry up and make whatever arrangements you can in the name of the Chief for transporting the body. Who can blame me for the kind of humor I started off in? I got out of the automobile at the door, stamping my feet, and blew into the big house like a tornado.

"Needless to say, my unexpected appearance in the room where they had laid out the dead man, who was fortunately covered with a sheet, was like a bomb. It paralyzed all the bunglers in charge of the situation there, beginning with the nuns' chaplain. Everyone stared at me open-mouthed. The silence and expectancy did not last long, however, for Angelo, the idiot, now grown into a big lout, but still drooling, came up to me laughing and pulling at my sleeve with grunts of joy. Of course I pushed him away. I had just noticed María Elena collapsed in an armchair in a corner with her hair uncombed and rings around her eyes. After a moment's thought I slowly went to her, bowed respectfully, took her by the hand, and gently but forcefully led her away from that atmosphere.

"No one dared to follow us, and I hadn't the vaguest notion what I was going to do from one moment to the next. That remained to be seen. I had not addressed a single word to her, and then, in the little side parlor, shaded against the hot glare of the midday sun by Venetian blinds, we stood alone in a corner of the room and I kept staring at her. Her appearance distressed me; but my mind was a blank. Then suddenly—bang!—she comes and throws herself on my neck and starts to weep convulsively.

"That upset me. What do you do in a case like that? I began to run my hand over her head (what else could I do?). Then suddenly she clamped her fingers on my arm and buried her face in my chest. She was exhausted, she had not slept, her breath was stale, and her beautiful eyes were swollen. I carried her to the sofa and went on caressing her. She put up no resistance whatever; in spite of the heat, her teeth were chattering. Actually she was half naked, with nothing but a dressing gown to cover her body. She kept staring at me in a stupor, but she made no resistance at all . . . Well, women are like that. After all, that sort of thing does calm their nerves.

"I don't know whether I did wrong or right, nor do I care. I covered her eyes with one hand to keep her from staring at me that way, stretched her out on the sofa to see if she could go to sleep, re-arranged her dressing gown, and, after also straightening myself, went back to the room where the dead man lay and found every troublesome task that could be imagined waiting for me.

"I made Angelo go away, too, for he was exasperating me with all his nonsense, and began to order the hundred thousand appropriate measures and dispositions, in the course of which the parish priest-nuns' chaplain was a great help to me. He is a poor stick of a man, but after all he was in his own alley. Actually, I had only to follow his suggestions (priests are the professionals of death), and with an order here and a telephone call there, everything was all organized and I made short work of the transportation of the body to the capital in a public health ambulance. Then, for my part, I could go back and report to the president that his wishes had been carried out. Then the matter passed over into the hands of the Under-Secretary of Public Instruction. The wake was to be held that same night for the upper echelons in one of the halls of the secretariat under his jurisdiction, the interment the following day, that is, today, with solemn funeral pomp.

"I have just come back from the cemetery. Bocanegra did not care to say good-bye to Dr. Rosales (he must have his reasons) at what the chancellor—the imbecile—in his flowery speech called 'the last abode.' There was no question but that the absence of the chief of state was bound to detract from the splendor of the ceremony. Indeed, more than one man, upon realizing it, spared himself the bother of following the cortège and sneaked away instead. Carmelo Zapata and Tuto Ramírez did that, for example, without any great attempt at dissimulation. They kept chatting as they let themselves be left behind, and then they weren't seen again."

CHAPTER

20

✦✦✦✦✦✦✦✦✦✦✦✦✦✦✦✦✦✦✦✦✦✦✦✦✦✦

What sort of comment does all this merit? I am
not going to make any. As the saying goes, "This, Inés, has
cleared away the muss—now never you mind about the fuss."
What I shall do, however, is to insert here as an addendum
some of the papers from the Convent of Santa Rosa in the village
of San Cosme which I am keeping on deposit until the man who
entrusted them to me shall reclaim them. They are letters and
first drafts of letters, a complete correspondence, which the
abbess had kept very neatly arranged in bundles tied with a
string, only to leave it all forgotten there in the anxiety of her
flight. Some of these papers deserve to be made known, and if
that is not to be—their publication when the time comes, I
mean—at any rate the points of view they offer will serve to
enlighten the historian in his evaluation of events.

For the time being I shall reproduce here two letters exchanged between the abbess and her relative, the widow of

Senator Rosales, wherein the abbess informs the other woman of the tragic end of her brother-in-law, Luisito. What the widow of the senator says in her reply clarifies some points of interest in retrospect after such a long time, and from a distance—she is now living with her children in the United States.

But first let us look at the skillfully written first draft by the abbess. It goes like this: "My dear Cousin: I have serious news to pass on to you today, for I seem to see [this brisk 'I seem to see' is inserted between the lines of the rough draft in the final wording] that it bears the unmistakable stamp of Divine Justice. Would you believe it? Your brother-in-law last night condemned himself to the same kind of death as the arch-betrayer Judas. Hence there can be no doubt in anyone's mind as to the motives for his past conduct, which some people are still trying to excuse by twisted sophistry and casuistry. He passed his own sentence and carried out upon himself that harsh and implacable punishment which leaves so few chances for Divine Mercy. And to think of the kind of man he was! Not even in that final hour of despondency, when he committed the most abominable of sins, did he have charity enough toward his own children to spare them such a frightful spectacle.

"This morning their wails, their grieving, their disturbance could be heard even inside the convent, for the Minister of Public Instruction had left his palaces and official mansions in the capital to come here to the village to take his life in the old family house, thereby besmirching the rooftree under which he was born and grew up with his parents and his older brother, your husband, may he rest in peace, and where his children were and still are, for they had come two or three weeks ago to spend the summer in San Cosme.

"You may well imagine, dear cousin, how excited my entire community was until they could find out what was going on, and how much trouble it caused me to calm these innocents [the word 'innocents' is written over the crossed-out word 'fools'], and I finally had to impose my authority to keep each in her place, they were so full of unhealthy curiosity to learn all the details. Even though it was probably labor lost, I ordered them to pray and ask God's Mercy on the wretched man, and I sent at once for Don Antonio, our chaplain, to establish contact with the house and take charge of everything. While he is on his way (the poor man is one of God's own, as you know, but he hasn't seen the light, and he is getting duller and duller with age) I am taking the opportunity to write you these hasty lines, for I'd rather the news would come to your ears through me than through some other agency. I feel sure that conflicting ideas and edifying reflections concerning the hidden and terrible designs of the Lord will spring to your mind, as they do to mine, while you learn what has happened. Only for a time does He permit iniquity to triumph in the world, perhaps as a punishment for the venial sins of those who are not so much wicked, thanks to Him. But sooner or later, when in His omniscience He considers the time right, He permits His divine anger to flash in a terrifying manner.

"I am planning to watch over those poor unfortunate orphans, especially María Elena, the daughter and your niece, who has been educated among us, for, as you know, the boy is not amenable to much of anything, and is nothing but a headache. In any case, it would be prudent to wait a while and see the course taken by events. It will not have escaped your attention that in such times as these, no caution is too great when one carries the responsibility for higher interests, which might be compromised in one way or another by any movement motivated by unreflecting good will. I must yet find the way to do this without detriment to those higher interests, but rather to their advantage."

The letter ended thus: "Well, Don Antonio has just come back to bring me up to date at last and then to return immediately to where he is so badly needed. My daughter, it is a horror. I must rush this off now, and later I shall write you again to keep you abreast of all that is happening."

The reply is much longer and contains some authoritative statements that have a bearing on later events. It covers several sheets, which are still to be found inside the envelope addressed from New York to the Reverend Mother Práxedes of the Sacred Heart of Mary, Superior in the Convent of Santa Rosa.

It begins: "Dear Cousin Práxedes: The only thing that occurs to me to say regarding the news of the death of that poor Luisito is: 'May God forgive Him!' And I say it from the heart; but I say it not as I should, out of goodness or as my Christian duty, but only out of weariness and a depth of indifference in myself which frightens me. When your prompt letter impressed on me what had happened, do you know that I felt not sorrow, nor surprise, nor even a recognition like yours of the hand of God, for perhaps I am not religious enough for that. I felt a kind of mortal weariness. Your letter reached me last Wednesday on one of those gray, dark, heavy, very depressing days that you there in the tropics can scarcely imagine. There, in our own country, it rains, in torrents indeed, and the rain can also last hours and hours at a time. But it is rain that has a hope! Your letter comes, and in one stroke everything surges come; it is something that supervenes. It's there and then suddenly it's gone, leaving the sky quite clear and the leaves on the trees glistening. And then people (as I remember and sigh for it), people who have been watching it like little animals from their holes, go out again rejoicing. Of course they can have no idea of what bad weather in New York is like. Perhaps I am exaggerating, or perhaps I have not yet adapted to it, and my children laugh at me; they don't understand me. Perhaps they don't even listen to me when I say that this world of stone, steel, and concrete is unreal, and that, for all its enormous pretensions, it comes unstuck in precipitation and fog.

"Well, it was one of those miserable days when I received your letter and I spent the entire afternoon crying. Suddenly the taste of the past was repeated on my palate, all that past which I had made such great efforts to cast into oblivion and to wipe out forever. But here it was again, in its entirety! Nothing is forgotten. How could it be? And still less whatever one would like to cover over at all costs. One fancies that one has managed to forge another life in this very different environment and lay the old one aside; or, at least, since I no longer count and that all that matters is the children, to cling tooth and nail to their future, which lies here, and to feed like a parasite on their hopes and prospects. That is what I live for, and as the past tells them nothing, I, too, have tried to wipe it from my horizon. But what up again, everything comes to the top again.

"When they came that night with their noise and their laughter, speaking to each other in English about something that had happened, they did not even notice that my eyes were still red in spite of the cold water in which I had bathed them. I was feeling the need to talk to them a little and had planned to do so, but hardly had I seen them come in, brimming over with other things, to sit down and devour the supper I had prepared for them as they argued with their mouths full over something or other on television, when I realized that there was no point in drawing them out of their world for a moment, for their's is the world of the streets, of their companions, and no longer my world. What could I say to them? That their uncle had died? That an old man, over there, had committed suicide? And what if I had? They would have stared at me in embarrassment, in stupefaction. Who knows what they would have thought of it, or what they would have said in reply so as to be able to turn their minds immediately to something else while I went on making a nuisance of myself? I chose not to speak to them; it would have been silly. After all, the healthiest thing for them is to be involved in their own doings.

"Later on, as I was going to bed, after they were both asleep, I went in to look at them, and the memory of that night when my poor Lucas entered their bedroom like that and stood contemplating them for a long time, tiny as they were then, caused a lump to rise in my throat. I had followed him and I could read in his face the stormy and bitter thoughts of that good-bye, but I had no means of opposing it or of finding any remedy for what was to come later. He had never spoken a single word to me concerning his plans, but why should he have? Didn't I know all about them? In any case, what other course was left to him? What arguments could I have used to dissuade him? I was looking at him, standing tall and strong and erect, full of his great virility; yet I was seeing him as a sick man doomed to die, as a man under sentence of death. I knew him far too well to believe that he had any other recourse. Not even I could suggest to him that he resign himself to such a way of life, so incompatible with his character. He was in a blind alley, back to the wall and there was no escape for him. You know very well, Práxedes, that for a man like him, in our country, there could be no other exit after what they had done to him. And when he finally put his pistol in his pocket and embraced me and left, I already knew, I had no doubt whatever, that he was going to his death even as I was longing to cling to the sight of him and to go with him to the capital to attend the senate sessions. Probably he would be killed and would kill in order to collect payment for that life which they had so treacherously stolen from him. I think he was prepared to do such courageous deeds in the capitol that he would give the lie to the mocking stares of the *canaille,* and so make clear that his virility had its roots in his heart and could not be wrenched from him without also pulling his heart out by the roots. What things, I don't know. Perhaps he himself did not know either. But, naturally, something quite spectacular. Hadn't a Mexican deputy blown the top off his own head several years ago right in the Chamber of Deputies? And hadn't the leader of the opposition in Havana shot himself in front of the radio microphone? Of course, that is the last resort. Who knows what other things Lucas might have been planning, things that might perhaps alter the course of events? His enemies understood perfectly when they learned that he was heading for the senate, and, emboldened by terror, they shot him down on the stairway so that he could not repeat Samson's feat, the feat of that great suicide, whose act, far from being vituperated, merits glorification in the Sacred Scriptures.

"Dear Práxedes, I have never before confided this to anyone, and I am confiding it to you today as to a sister, in order to unburden my heart. Human acts, as you know, cannot be judged apart from their motivations and circumstances. If they are, they amount to nothing. Who would dare to condemn my husband's decision, a decision perfectly in keeping with the nobility of his character, and almost obligatory because of it? That being so, I ask myself what motives his brother Luis could have had now. In accordance with his own character, that wretch had made up his mind to accept the diminished, decadent, unworthy existence that my Lucas had rejected. Surely in that sense circumstances drove him to it. Perhaps he had thought he could find a compromise, that he could swim and keep his clothing dry—I don't know. I pity him for his twistedness, especially right now when he has shown that he was not such a base soul after all, for in the end he was not able to live without dignity either. Each person's nature is his own and each follows his own bent. In the midst of my misfortunes, I am proud to know that my husband never hesitated a moment, and that perhaps he did not hesitate because he felt sure of me. That night, before our sleeping children, he was able to read in my eyes not only that I admired him and that I approved of his conduct in advance, for all my sorrow, but also that, once he had been struck down, I would take away our children in all haste and with an energy to equal his own. Our two little savages are here, quite beautiful, making their way in a much wider world.

"But what about his brother's circumstances? Lucas died according to his law, and Luis according to his. Sometimes the cultivation of the intelligence and study will serve only to weaken the will, to cause it to go astray and finally to make the wrong move after a great deal of caviling. I feel sure that the unfortunate man made his mistakes through weakness, possibly even because of overly delicate feelings. You needn't be surprised at this opinion. I can already see your gesture of protest; but I am not mad and I know what I am saying. Of all those mistakes, I consider his suicide the gravest, the least pardonable, but at the same time, the most deserving of compassion. It is as if Lucas, his older brother, had attempted to evade his destiny, to disguise reality, only to have to hang himself years later, humbled and conquered. To a certain extent, something of that sort may have happened to Luisito, it seems to me. For all his talent, he was a deluded man, a completely deluded man, and at heart a simple soul, full of romanticism. May God forgive him for the wrong he has done to himself, and for what he has done to his children!

"*À propos* of them, you tell me, cousin, that you are thinking of looking out for the girl. Without a doubt that will be the best thing for her. The one who worries me more is the boy. I think I may be able to pluck up the courage to take him myself. My boys would be delighted to have him, though that might be only as a novelty. And so, in the pinch, we all may be able to go ahead."

CHAPTER

21

++++++++++++++++++++++++++

This lady ends her letter by asking her cousin, the abbess, to keep her informed.

Before going any farther, I should like to make clear how those papers came into my hands, and that means giving some of the local incidents that were stirred up in the village of San Cosme by the revolution started at the National Palace with the assassination of the president.

To judge by the unexpected manner—I might even say the comic manner, because it was so easy—in which those documents came into my hands, and to judge further by the carefully chosen words that accompanied their delivery—that I was the person best suited to keep them in his custody, almost the pre-destined one, so to speak—one's wish might be said to possess some mysterious force with which to evoke what his imagination has pictured as his heart's desire. For the truth is that my efforts to collect and fill out the documentation needed for my historical work played no part whatsoever in this acquisition. To be sure, other harvests have been reaped owing to my vigilance, but they had come to me as the result of cunning, great effort, and risk. One example of this is that after the Spanish legation had been characterized as the "den of the hydra of reaction" owing to persistent rumors and references in *El Comercio* (new era) and had been subjected to an assault by the rabble, I had maneuvered to meet, impress, and win over the sergeant-major responsible for the custody of the building, and thus had managed to get from him permission to enter the building, so that I, in my turn, could ransack the already half-scattered archives, although my motives were not destructive—quite the opposite. But these other papers dropped on me from the sky. And if I say they dropped from the sky, that is because a minister of God, no less, a priest, actually a saint, came to hand them over to me when I should least have expected that. This good man was Don Antonio, the parish priest of Santa Rosa and the convent chaplain.

But as is often the case with other miracles, this one can be explained very simply. Pure chance is the explanation. Chance decreed that a certain Malagarriga among the nuns at Santa Rosa, a distant relative of mine on my mother's side whom I could remember only very vaguely, but who had seemingly remembered me very well, had given my name to the priest when that holy man had had to drive the frightened little lambs to the capital in a light truck after the abbess had fled.

"The abbess," the pastor explained to me, "had disappeared in the middle of the uproar as if swallowed up by the earth, leaving all of them . . ."—those were his words—". . . floundering in the greatest consternation." No one knew what fate might have befallen her and conjecture had even gone so far as to wonder whether the attackers had not kidnapped her and carried her off as a hostage. Consequently, it was a great relief to him when finally, but not until the following morning, they heard the telephone ring in the sacristy and recognized her imperious voice. They could hear her shrieking into the instrument that she was calling from the capital, from the Spanish legation, where she had sought sanctuary; that she had hastened there in order to beg asylum for the member of her community with the required urgency, "and to obtain it, naturally," and that she had been busy getting ready for their installation—a serious problem, for they were no mere two or three—until such time as they could be evacuated. The Reverend Mother issued her instructions immediately. The nuns were to be transferred to the legation without the loss of a moment's time and under his most strict superintendence.

"Just imagine it," the priest said to me. "They are certainly not two or three, and everything had to be improvised. At last Señor Luna, a Spaniard who conducts several branches of business in San Cosme, agreed to lend me his old light truck. Then I had to find someone to drive it, and so the poor little things went like lambs to the slaughter, while I was trembling as I sat next to the driver for fear that something might happen along the way. All that, only to find that when we thought we were arriving at the portal of salvation, the legation had been sacked during the night, too, and could no longer offer any safety to anyone. Of course it was taken for granted that, thanks to God, the abbess was already across the border. Finally I succeeded in sloughing off the burden of my responsibility upon the vicar of the diocese. He was in a vile humor and spoke to me in harsh words that, frankly, I don't think I deserved, but he did take charge of the nuns and has settled them in small groups here and there."

"Harsh words?" I asked him.

Yes, it seemed that the vicar had gone so far as to talk about meager vocations for martyrdom, and had added—in general terms of course, and grumbling all the while—an imputation of stupidity and pusillanimity. My interlocutor had realized, however, that in such a situation everyone was feeling nervous. He himself never stopped staring with every sign of anxiety first at the ceiling, then at the window, all the while mopping his brow with his handkerchief as he was talking to me.

"Well, in my humble opinion, my dear sir, you have done everything that could be done and more," I assured him, and he gazed at my face with a half incredulous gratitude, looking calmer and almost happy.

Then he handed me the portfolios, which he had been holding in his lap tightly grasped in both hands. With great solemnity he placed those papers in my care, saying that he had believed that he ought to collect them from the pigeonholes in the desk of the mother superior before the expedition set forth. He supposed they might be of some interest, but in any case, what could he do with a legacy like that? He did not want to leave them there, exposed to the danger of falling into who knows whose hands. Now he could go back immediately to San Cosme. The chauffeur was waiting for him on the parade ground; and of course he had no fear at all that his name would become engraved on the roll of martyrs. That was a lot of nonsense, but as the vicar had proved so intractable, he begged me—for he had known perfectly all along precisely who I was, thanks to my relative—he begged me to keep those papers, even thought they might prove in the end to be without interest.

And so it was that those documents chanced to fall from the sky into the hands of this Little Pinedo, your servant, who was rubbing those same hands with glee. I urged my caller to have dinner with me, and he thanked me for my insistence. He had not had a bite to eat, now that he thought of it, since . . . since when? Ah, yes, since nearly twenty-four hours before, what with the trip and all the worry, plus the disagreeable surprise of his arrival and the displeasure of the vicar; and then, later, trying to find me, for he had not had my address, only my name. Luckily my personal features . . . He was a little perturbed . . . In short, he had learned by asking that I was a very well-known person, and he had located me easily.

"But how did the convent happen to be attacked? Was there anything that might have led anyone to expect it?" I asked him as he sat facing me, avidly devouring a couple of fried eggs and a lot of bread.

"Nothing, absolutely nothing. True, the atmosphere in the village had become strange after the arrival of the news of Bocanegra's violent death. Still, nothing at all had happened during the first three or four days. Then it came. One morning the body of a man, a certain neighbor, one López, was found hanging head down like a hen at the very spot where rumor had it that a barbarous deed had been done to Senator Lucas Rosales some time earlier. Perhaps you may not know, Señor Pinedo," the priest added—and I did not say yes or no—"perhaps you may not know that the one who was blamed for it was that particular man, Chino López, and it seems that he himself had even bragged of it. Surely someone had it in for him, but frankly, no matter from what angles I examine the case, I haven't the least notion who it could have been or who they could have been. Nor does it seem to me that anyone else has the vaguest idea. But the whole village sensed that it was an act of reprisal, more or less connected with the Big House.

"Now, you will remember that the Big House was vacant after the death of Dr. Rosales, the minister, who committed suicide there. No one knew for sure whether the immovable property was in the custody of the court, or how the matter lay; but the fact is that the girl had gone to live in the convent before they sent her abroad. After all, what do I know about it? The one thing certain is that the abbess was very much tied to the owners by blood relationship and friendship. But, for all that, no one had foreseen the attack. Who could have? And besides, I feel sure that it was not cooked up in the village. The people who carried it out, at least, were all strangers, outsiders. The posse arrived on horseback, not charging in, but walking, and one of them was singing one of those insolent songs which are being heard everywhere nowadays, and they did not start to behave improperly or wheel their horses and fire their guns or frighten people until they reached the small plaza. Finally, when not a soul could be seen anywhere, they began to let out frightful yells, and at the word 'Now!' they stormed the gate. They forced it and all of them to the last man poured through the opening, still on their horses.

"Then the indescribable happened; they made a stable of the garden and turned to sacking and stealing to their heart's content. Fortunately, there were no profanations or sacrileges; nor can the nuns complain about the integrity of their persons, but only of the terrible fright they experienced, and of being given a shove now and then. Destruction, yes, that they left, as much as they pleased, and when they had had enough, off they went again on horseback. They rode off into the country shouting 'Long live the poor!' with no one to say them nay. There were more than twenty of them. They were wearing black skulls painted on their big straw hats. What no one has been able to verify up to this moment," Don Antonio concluded as he wiped up the olive oil on his plate with a piece of bread, "is how the abbess managed to slip away so quickly in the midst of that uproar, and I ask myself how she could manage to flee to the capital. Although it was rumored immediately that the bandits had carried her off to be ransomed, no one was sure that he had seen her among them, and many a pair of eyes was spying on the departure of the attackers from behind closed shutters. It seems to me that she could perhaps have escaped through the orchard, and it's possible that some automobile passing by on the road may have taken her away from the village. Surely she must have believed that those barbarians were about to chop off all their heads."

In a way, I was wishing that my visitor would leave so that I could find out the sooner what the folder of papers contained; something kept telling me it was to be a great surprise, and, in any case, I am a curious man. But in another way, I wanted to ask him some more questions, aimed at clearing up certain details related to those people and events. Among those details was the whereabouts of the Rosales children whose father had been the cabinet member, for it seemed to me I had heard mentioned in passing that the girl was abroad. The good man pondered a while, fetched up a small sigh, and made known to me with some circumlocution that after the daughter had stayed a while in the convent, the abbess had indeed sent her to New York in the care of her aunt, the senator's widow. But he could not give me any accurate information about the boy, poor thing. Now if I would excuse him, he had to start for San Cosme; the chauffeur must be in despair. Certainly. But I hoped that he, at least, had not been subjected to any inconveniences in the exercise of his ministry. As he stood near the door, he gave me his assurance that up to then he had not, thank God. The only serious happening in the village up to then had been what was done to Chino López and, even more serious, the attack on the convent, but other unpleasant annoyances had not been lacking, to be sure. The mayor (who had already spent an eternity in office, if the truth be told) had been dispossessed summarily, and another character had been put in his place—a man no worse, though very stupid indeed, but as the municipal secretary had not been ousted, that did not matter much. Aside from some protests and outcries, some stupid performances and some lowering of the general tone, everything remained basically the same.

He lingered a moment, then added before leaving: "Do you want to know something, Señor Pinedo? If they hadn't hanged Chino López head down, perhaps he would be mayor now. So you try to figure out the designs of Providence."

C H A P T E R

22

   The priest from San Cosme finally left, and I lost
no time in opening the portfolios he had left with me and taking
out what they contained. In addition to invoices and receipts
and other papers of negligible interest, I came upon the legacy
of letters to which the two earlier transcripts herein belong,
plus some school exercise books that instantly drew my attention. They were carefully tied with a sky-blue ribbon and
written in a fine hand along the blue lines. Insofar as they are
pertinent, I am going to reproduce their text here and now. As
we shall see, it consists of some anguished, almost convulsed
pages that María Elena, the daughter of Luisito Rosales, had
written following her father's suicide. Despite the suffering, the
perturbation, and the anxiety that impregnate them, and a kind
of rhetoric she had inherited or learned at home, those pages
seem to me to mirror the qualities of a noble soul. Her phrases

are childish at times, but isn't there something of maturity and even of an adult repentance that transcends everything?

"I have cried all night, but have found no relief" are the first words in that part of the notebook, coming immediately after an old composition on the sunset in the tropics, quite conventional and characterized by the painstaking wordiness of the pupil, which is in contrast to the agitation and passion of the writing that follows.

"I had thought," she goes on, "that tears might unburden my heart, but it has not happened that way; I have wept the whole night, but have found no consolation. And now that morning has come, I have no more tears. To keep from losing my mind, I looked in the bottom of a drawer for my notebook, forgotten among my schoolbooks, and I shall try to explain myself to myself, now that I have no one in the world to whom I can confide, the burden that weighs me down. Dear notebook: why have you, too, contrived to afflict me with the irony of those nonsensical things you've been guarding from the past, from another I, now gone, never to return? At least help me! At least you . . . but, alas, it would be better for me to organize what has happened, instead of wearing myself out with side issues that instantly sound hollow to myself.

"The facts are hard, hard but very exact, and I shall devote myself to them. One fact is that at last, thank God, they managed to relieve me of my burden, to let me pass it on. The sound of a motor down below in the street and the pitying faces surrounding me announce the departure of the ambulance, carrying him away. In line with his duties as parish priest and spiritual guardian, Don Antonio came to me then, and placed a comforting hand on my shoulder. I seized it desperately and told him that I would like him to hear my confession. Suddenly I felt the urge to confess, and I told him so, that I should like to make my confession straightaway. His face showed his stupefaction. With some alarm, he tried to put it off until the following day, after I had rested and calmed down somewhat. But I was calm. My throat was dry, but I was quite calm. I insisted and insisted. I pressed him so that he had no choice but to agree to hear me.

[162]

"We went to sit down on the sofa in the little parlor. On that very sofa, dear God! And what I had to confess to him was certainly enough to frighten the poor man. He thought at first that I was confused by grief and that perhaps my mind was wandering. That was how absurd what I had to tell him must have seemed to him. But when he was convinced that I was lucid, that things were precisely as I said, the good man was dumfounded. And why shouldn't he be disconcerted and terribly consternated at that monstrous deed that I—the naïve little girl whom he had known since childhood—was relating to him in bald terms, without dressing it up at all? I told him that with my father not cold yet, only two steps away from the place where his poor body was lying, I behind the door had given mine to the first stranger, as the worst kind of light woman might have done. As I live, I can hardly believe it myself! It seems to me more as if I am struggling in the chains of a stubborn nightmare, that it is all impossible and a lie, and that finally, when God wills me to awaken, I shall find—to my infinite relief—that I am still as virgin as before, and that my unhappy father has not perpetrated that horror upon himself.

"But not so, for the nightmare is lasting too long and I have been crying through the whole of this night. It actually has happened; it is not a bad dream, and no one can wipe it out or undo it now. Why shouldn't good Don Antonio be frightened? I was expecting some tremendous reaction from his judgment seat, something adequate to the gravity of my infamy. I wanted such a reaction and was waiting for it with a kind of hopeful anxiety. But instead of that, the unhappy man kept staring at me with the eyes of a sheep for a time that seemed to me endless, and when he recovered from his astonishment, it was only to subject me to a questioning that was vacillating and sluggish because of his perturbation. The poor man was even more beaten down than I was; it almost seemed that he was the penitent. When he had managed to fit the unlikely story into the frame of reality with the aid of the most odiously concrete details, he said: 'Pray, pray hard, my daughter,' which is all that occurred to him, and in the end his embarrassment added to my forlornness.

"It was abominable; it was as if I had been forced to go through that experience for the second time. I had composed my confession in terse, truthful terms, the fewest possible, only the indispensable ones. I had made the effort, swallowed hard, and then poured it all out in flood. But as he was listening to me, he wore on his face the expression of a man who has been actually watching the serpent symbolizing sin issue from my mouth. And as he could not believe his own eyes, he tortured me with questions that forced me to specify each one of the horrible details, brought forth in cold blood and in a harsh light without the anesthesia of stupefaction or the dark excitement that had taken possession of me at the time of my downfall. It was as if I could feel the hands of a clumsy surgeon rummaging through my insides. He wanted to know the name of the scoundrel (indignation drove him to use that designation from his holy seat of judgment), and when I had spoken it, when I had named Tadeo, I could not hold back a weak smile at his reaction, no matter how painful the moment. 'But Tadeo is not a stranger,' he protested. 'You told me it was a stranger.'

"In the heat of accusing myself I had said that. But, indeed, Tadeo was not a stranger: Don Antonio was right. And I must admit that when I saw him make his unexpected entrance into the parlor where I had collapsed and was smothering, and saw him approach me without any hesitation, and take me by the hand, and lead me out of there with such firm assurance, I admit that I felt at that moment—I admit it!—that he was the only one left me in the world, absurdly enough, my only and ultimate hold on salvation.

"I am trying to search out my hidden springs, trying not to deceive myself with false excuses. I know very well that there is no excuse for me, but at least I should like to make clear before my own court of justice who I am, so as to be able to detest myself to my very depths. For the truth is that I, only I, and not he, am the stranger; a stranger whose presence, whose existence, I had never even suspected, and who has revealed herself suddenly, incomprehensibly, inside myself. Don Antonio will have to exhaust his pious platitudes in vain. When I think over what I have done, how I yielded myself without any resistance whatsoever, without even an inward resistance, I cannot rid myself of the idea that I might have given myself in that way at any moment, always, as soon as the idea had occurred to him and—what is still more terrifying—that I would do the same thing again tomorrow, right now, should he appear and want me to. That's what I am, then. That's what I am. Suddenly I have discovered myself. At the same time I also have discovered him.

"So he wasn't a stranger? He wasn't a stranger? What did it matter that during the boredom on my eternal balcony he had diverted me since I was a little girl with his comings and goings, with his silly adolescent acting-up in front of the other poor boys, of whom he was the ringleader and whom he bossed, and that I had to fall back on my dull reading, on taking care of Angelo, more nervous than usual at such times, and that I used to envy them their freedom on those afternoons when they did not chance to come to play in front of the house? Nor does it matter that later, when we were living in the capital, my father used to bring him home from time to time, with that spontaneous and excessive hospitality of his, which I could not approve of, or rather which made me feel humiliated and tense. Was he any less a stranger for all that? Any less an insufferable and pretentious man? I think I even came to hate the very name of Tadeo from having heard his praises sung by my father. An extraordinary talent, he would say and then emphasize it: ex-tra-or-di-na-ry, and deserving of every encouragement and stimulus. And I would stubbornly keep still, furious, knowing that he was asking me to contradict him, put up any little objection at all so that he could reason with me endlessly and try to justify himself. I knew that he would undoubtedly flatten me with his arguments. And for that very reason, I kept still. I closed the door on him. I refused him that small charity; I nursed my inner intransigence. Innocence is implacable; it's despicable. Too late one comes to repent of one's cruelty! Only after there is no second chance. Why, O Lord, do You not permit us to correct our drawing, do our embroidery over, wipe out our worst mistakes? There's no help for it now; there is never any remedy for what truly matters.

"My eyes are open—the opening of my flesh has also served to open my eyes—and I wish the earth would swallow me up. How could I really have loved my poor father, seeing that I did not know him either? My affection was nothing but what is called a regrettable mistake. That filial love of mine, slightly rancorous, slightly resentful, remote, respectful, but above all distant, was bound to turn into a kind of carnival burlesque of a heart so undone by tribulations and vacillations. He was alone; he had me beside him, but he was alone. With his head bowed and his hands behind his back, he used to pace and pace the room endlessly, and, as if the incessant mobility of Angelo was not enough to wear on my nerves, seeing him do that again and again used to exasperate me. I would never answer his casual reflections, and I used to let him feel my irritation until he would stop walking the floor and go away, tired out.

"He was alone, always alone. When Mama died, she blocked up for us both whatever matter there was for dispute between him and me, and made it taboo. Hadn't there been plenty of ground for argument? Anything he would do, plan, or propose, she would instantly oppose, and she would attack him directly, curtly, and even a little brutally, for that was natural to her sincere character. I can see it all so clearly now! In the final analysis, what she was disapproving, criticizing and condemning was not this or that act of his, but the man himself. With no great love to hinder her, she was rejecting him from the depths of her being. They were as irreconcilable as fire and water. He would have had to annihilate himself! And that is what he has done now —rubbed himself out. One may learn suddenly all the terrible rightness there can be in a vulgar expression: he has rubbed himself out. Wasn't that what she had always wanted, without knowing it? Well, she has achieved it at least, and—my hand is shaking as I write it—it was through my agency, at least in part. I served as her instrument. When she died, she made everything that meant going contrary to her clear, limpid, noble, simple, immovable, stern criteria seem like sacrilege, and I could not approve my father's subtleties without feeling that I was betraying and offending her memory, even though I could understand him, as I did understand very well the private reasons behind his acts and the whole reason for his conduct. It was incumbent upon me—it weighed upon me—like a sacred duty to challenge him; and I used to experience a kind of bitter pleasure in doing so.

"Hadn't she said, once and for all, that Bocanegra was a rascal? Well, I subscribed to that judgment with my eyes closed, and no imaginable considerations to the contrary were of any avail: such considerations as that, rascal though he was, he had still belonged to a decent family, that nothing could be proved concerning who was responsible for the death of Uncle Lucas despite the proper coroner's inquest and the promises made to my father. Furthermore, there could be no doubt that if my father had taken an intransigent stand, we would not have kept our house and the little that was left to us, and no one knows what would have become of us, of the unfortunate Angelo and me.

"Now, and only now, in the face of the accomplished fact, I can begin to appreciate the anxieties he must have suffered, my poor father, as he shuffled his own perplexities together under the steady pressure of his wife, who could not have felt the problem so dramatically or so acutely, for Uncle Lucas was not her brother, only her brother-in-law. And besides, she had never been on the best of terms with his widow. It did not cause her much grief to see my aunt leave finally, to take her chances, with a child clinging to each hand. Of course, my father managed to see that they had an automobile escort to the border, and he made certain financial arrangements for her which would enable her to get along. All this is worth taking into account. But the sentence remained unchanged: Bocanegra was a rascal, and when my mother died, it was my duty to uphold that judgment with all its consequences, even though no one had told me to do it. The consequences add up to an inflexible attitude, actually an inhuman one, toward the highly complicated world in which my father had to maneuver. Bocanegra a rascal—just that. And

Tadeo, an insolent mulatto. Did I have to listen to her? I was as sure of this opinion of hers as if I could hear it issue from her thin, tight lips. From beyond the grave, she kept sending forth her peremptory, unappealable judgments on people. And it fell to me to formulate them for her. An ex-tra-or-di-na-ry talent, my father used to proclaim, while inwardly I would answer him: an insolent mulatto. Not I—she, from inside me. She, with her fine, imperturbable, simple certainty. Who would have said then, seeing her so sure of herself, full of that wholehearted energy, that her days were numbered and her life was drawing to an end? Today they are both beneath the ground, and I am alone here forever, until I can go to join them. May God have mercy on their souls!

"Alas, I am wandering helplessly. I am lost, and I don't want to read over what I have written. What good would it do? This confession, this undirected scream, ought to help me, for that was its purpose, to collect my thoughts, which have been wandering, twisting and running together whenever I throw myself into the armchair with my eyes closed, these burning eyes, dry now for all eternity.

" 'But how could you, my daughter? Why did you let yourself do it?' poor Don Antonio kept asking me in consternation, with more perplexity than reproach in his voice. As if I could have any reply to give him! As if that were not the very question I keep asking myself and asking myself again, tirelessly, and always with stupefaction. I know we live surrounded by mystery, that the entire universe is impenetrable, and that we have no recourse but to bow before the Divine Greatness. But there is nothing so terrifying as to realize that one's own depths are also impenetrable, as not to know one's self, to be ignorant of what one is. I remember, I shall never forget, the fright that took possession of me when, still within the realm of childhood, the first flow of blood appeared suddenly and cried out of a filth in my body. How could I, poor creature, be responsible for it? But I had already been taught to despise the body, to distrust it, to be ashamed of it. The body, with all its daily humiliations, was the dwelling place which Our Lord Jesus Christ had accepted in order to show us the way through His example, and to teach us to get along with the beast without detriment to the spirit. Yes, the spirit has always been here, to save the situation. But what if the spirit suddenly rebels, too, leaves home, gets away? What if the spirit also turns out to be an unruly animal that does not recognize you and will not obey your call, and looks at you, mocking and strange but never comes within reach of your hand?

"I ask myself why I did what I did; and I have no answer. Who am I, then? I was awake and I knew perfectly well what was going on, especially as after his first soft but forcefully persuasive caresses, he went on to handle me brutally and insolently. There could be no doubt; there was no room to deceive myself. I knew, and I consented. Not only did I content; I abandoned myself with the delight that must be experienced by one who finally yields in exhaustion to the waters or who, having lost his final refuge, reconciles himself with death and stands motionless waiting for the tiger to spring and devour him. In reality his eyes were not bold, but inhuman rather; he was watching me with the terrible, unmoved indifference of a beast sure of the prey beneath its paw. And I, in the midst of my abjectness, confusion, and scorching heat, was experiencing a rare happiness, the happiness of realizing that I was lost beyond recall.

"Now I see that I am lost and dishonored, but as I can give no reason for my behavior, I cannot find the road to repentance either. All I feel is astonishment at myself. I don't know myself. I don't know who I am. That is all there is to it. I have not even left my crushed confessor, poor old man, the recourse of shedding divine mercy upon me by granting me absolution, for I could not tell him that I repented. I didn't, and I don't. Sad, exhausted, annihilated I am, yes, but not penitent. Why not? Well, because in spite of my compliance, I view what has happened as something beyond my reach. The loss of my virginity and the suicide of my father are mingled in my mind, and they weigh on me like one single sin that precedes any thought of mine, but for which I must answer without its having been humanly possible to avoid."

CHAPTER

23

✦✦✦✦✦✦✦✦✦✦✦✦✦✦✦✦✦✦✦✦✦✦✦✦✦

As the sophisticated and discreet reader will have recognized immediately, this wise child discovered quite by accident, although at great cost to herself, poor girl, that frightening midland which is Original Sin. The preceding pages, so agitated, so rhetorical at times, are the result of indigestion from eating of the famous apple of Eden. (But who has decreed that rhetoric is incompatible with sincerity? It is not, but on the contrary may serve to re-enforce it.)

I must confess, nonetheless, that some of her anguished thoughts gave me something to ponder as I was reading them. If you, lovely child, have rejected your body, and if the filth of your physiology humiliates you, if at times you young girls are ashamed, for example, of the ostentatious development of your young breasts, as is frequently the case, what is there to say about it? Well, what can I say? Among those who occupy themselves with the authentic iconography of Jesus—what nonsense—there are some who maintain that Our Saviour was actually crippled or deformed, too. Wasn't it enough, perhaps, for Him to have become a man?

But to go back to María Elena. She spent only a few weeks in the Convent of Santa Rosa. The letter from the abbess that I shall copy later tells something about her immediate fate. In general, the rough copies by the abbess show few corrections. One of them is so nearly perfect, indeed, that it seems more like the final copy. As a rule she would change a detail here or there when she made her fair copy, but the drafts each seem to have been written at one sitting, and almost all of them could have gone as original letters except for some small emendation.

That did not happen, however, with the next letter she addressed to her cousin in New York, the widow of Senator Rosales. It was the exception. In it she was asking her to take charge of María Elena, and she was trying to do it in such a way that the widow would be left no room to object, and no choice but to accept the accomplished fact, however reluctantly. She had to rephrase that letter a thousand times before she could achieve her final copy, as the rough draft that I have testifies. Literally, it is overrun with crossed-out words, insertions, transpositions and other changes. But in the end it must have been edited enough and must have reached its destination more or less in the following terms:

"I feel very distressed, dear cousin, to have had to make the decision I am about to tell you about, as well as at the displeasure I must inevitably cause you. My own has been no less, as you will understand when you realize what this deals with. What I must tell you straightaway, without any preamble, and somewhat brutally is this: you must know that your niece, that angel face of a María Elena, has deceived us all and has turned out to be a shameless lost soul. I mean just that. You may struggle against believing that, I know; I myself have the proof before my eyes and can hardly believe it. But that is how it is, and before I go on I want to give you my word, so that there can be no doubt, that the proofs are in my possession, in the most unmistakable form in the world, a statement written in her own hand. Are you surprised? You may guess, then, what was my surprise when I found such abominations in a notebook that I had taken away from her, as was my duty.

"After all the sisters were asleep, she was spending hours by herself, I give you my word, and as soon as I learned of that, I decided to search her belongings to find out what she was up to, for I must watch over them all. My child, you cannot imagine such filth. What that vulgar girl was writing consisted of verses upon verses, idiocies. But in the midst of all that nonsense, I suddenly found a relation, a kind of very cynical confession in which that infant takes delight in things that might bring a blush to the cheek of a cavalry sergeant. I swear it. To make a long story short—for I'd like to pass over it holding my nose because it stinks—as I said above, she herself declares that she is a lost soul and is even pleased to characterize herself by the term of fallen woman.

"And here am I, the one who brought her, misled by a worthy intention, to live with these innocents in the bosom of a community that was and always must be the seat of the most unblemished purity! God forgive me for having exposed them to the contamination of sin in such a fashion! In all humility—for, as you know, I never mind taking the blame—I acknowledge that I had been overly imprudent and that the unbelievable hypocrisy of that girl does not excuse me. I ought to have considered her family background, and I blame myself for not having done so. I should have realized that something disturbing, dark, demoniac, in short, must be in the blood of a man who added suicide to treason, even though you, dear cousin, can find it in your heart to look for excuses for everything. And what later happened to the boy (already so marked by the hand of God with his congenital imbecility) should have forewarned me and taught me to be cautious. Idiot though he is, he found it no problem to escape from the village so as to elude the discipline he was to have been placed under until some other arrangements could be made for him. Why would his sister be any better?

"Perhaps I am letting myself be carried away, dear cousin, by

[173]

the indignation aroused in me by the discovery of this mess, and perhaps I am exaggerating. But the fact remains, and about that there can be no question, that this unfortunate girl cannot stay in the convent any longer. I called Don Antonio up on the carpet (for this is another chapter, I can assure you) and gave him such a piece of my mind that his ears were scorched. He had no right to do what he did (as I say, this is another chapter that I shall tell you about some day), and I ordered him to make all the arrangements for your niece to leave for New York immediately.

"I feel sure, as I know you so well, that you will approve of my decision, and that you will be glad that I have adopted it without any loss of time. Actually, I don't believe I had any other alternative. A scandal would have had repercussions all through the convent in the most regrettable way, and that must be avoided. Lest anyone think a scandal would be implicit in making any other decision, we have decided to defray the expenses of the trip out of our scanty resources, and to send her to you because you said in the beginning that you were disposed to give a home to Angelo, the brother. Now I must ask you to help us to straighten out the mess in this way. The girl is your relative, however undeserving of it, and she has got us into the mess. Naturally, I can't expect you to receive her in your home, particularly as you have sons. But it should be easy for you to find some job for her. She knows English well, and no one could fail to know how they carry on there in that country when it comes to morals; all cats are gray at night, and it would be better for her to have to shift for herself.

"By the time you receive this letter, I calculate that everything will be planned and ready. I shall send you a wire as soon as that jewel starts for New York so that you can meet her and take charge of her."

CHAPTER

24

++++++++++++++++++++++++++++

I think that when the time comes for me to sit down and edit the text of my history in all seriousness, some of these things may be left out or cut down to a brief mention. Actually, I don't know why I have given them so much play, even here in this unorganized assemblage of documents and news items. Perhaps it would have been sufficient to condense them into the brief space of a couple of lines and to say that, as an outgrowth of the suicide of Dr. Rosales, his daughter María Elena was taken into the Convent of Santa Rosa and later transferred to the care of an aunt of hers in New York, while Angelo, the boy, disappeared from the village. Even such data as those are hardly worth putting down in writing; *mutatis mutandi,* that is how great families always end, leaving the trumpets of fame no reason to peal forth their inglorious coda.

Let us go back, then, to the memoirs of Tadeo Requena, our main source, and pick them up again at a critical point. As a matter of fact, the manuscript breaks off for a time following his mordant commentaries on the obsequies for the Minister of Public Instruction. Doubtless he must have spent several days suffering a crisis, which might be called one of conscience, except that it would be exaggerating to attribute a conscience to this sinister character of ours. Whatever happened, he stopped his scribbling for a time, and from then on we find in his prose very few of these digressions, minutiae, or even niggling that the writer-secretary used to indulge in, and of which I have shown some examples here. No, from then on, he goes straight to the heart of the matter, without definitively abandoning his style, of course (for it has been said, and by no one less than a naturalist, that the style is the man). He restricts himself to what matters, instead of amusing himself by meandering through thickets, as he had seemed earlier to delight in doing. Or perhaps there is no change in attitude; it may be that the increasingly serious course of affairs, merely by being there, shut off his chances for vague literary diversion. In any case, we know for certain that young Tadeo's pen races as if a pack of hounds were at his heels. And as we shall see, the pack caught up with him in the end.

But first let us go on with the editing of his memoirs and see what he left behind him after that pause. Tadeo Requena writes: "I left off these notes of mine, or whatever they are, for a number of days, and now I find myself clumsy at tying them together again, for I no longer know whether or not there is any point in doing that. I started them as an amusement, out of vanity, perhaps, and I keep on with them almost as a penance, like one of those labors undertaken with the aim of saving the soul. Where were we? Too many things have happened, and there are times when I feel fed up, satiated, sated with everything. The truth is that I cannot see the exit from this labyrinth clearly, and cannot even imagine what it will turn out to be. The one sure thing—I hate to admit this to myself, but why deceive myself?—the one sure thing is that that woman is doing as she likes with me. I detest and despise her, and I have not hesitated to let her know it, but still she does as she likes with me. I think that perhaps what overpowers me is her boldness, that her very folly subjugates me. From the beginning I have known only too well that I would have to defend myself against her, and yet she has managed to drag me after her, even though when I am alone, I am in despair at having been brought to accede to what I don't want, what doesn't interest me, what doesn't suit me. And yet that is exactly how it has been from the first moment. I have refrained from setting this down in writing as it was happening: it is unbecoming, it is shameful, and it depresses me a great deal. But now I must put it down in black and white, against any eventuality."

Requena goes on to tell in detail how he came to have congress with and carnal knowledge of the First Lady of the Republic. I shall not copy the pages in his own terms, however juicy a morsel they are to me, all the more delicious in contrast to the heavy, angry tone he adopts in his account. According to him, it was Doña Concha who propositioned her husband's young secretary, and certainly in a very abrupt manner, after having failed in several earlier attempts, or, if you like, after dropping hints. This time she went up to his desk on the pretext of trying to read what he was writing. She leaned both hands on the corner of the desk and let the overflowing contents of her ample bodice fall forward. "She even let me see what the sun never shines on!" Tadeo brutally declares. And that sight must have been the signal for the *sursum corda,* for he rose from his chair and said to her: "See here, *Señora,* no one plays games with me. I must tell you that I am not the chaste Joseph!" The First Lady then deliberately put out her hand, so he says, and touched him where she should not have, then exclaimed with a loud laugh: "Good God! So that's the way things stand!" "So one is young!" Tadeo protests.

Young, yes, but not completely lacking in self-control, for he goes on to explain: "As she dodged my grab at her hand, and went away with her leisurely, swaying walk, I was given the opportunity to get hold of myself and let her see, when she turned around to send me an inviting laugh from the doorway, that I was not running after that awful bitch like a lap dog. I was going to let her find out who I was. I was determined to humble her, although after thinking it all over and weighing and measuring everything quite carefully, I decided to take a leaf from history, which is the teacher of life, and especially from sacred history. Though I am no chaste Joseph, indeed I am not, I should not care to suffer the fate of that just man either. I was able more or less to carry out the plan I outlined for myself: never to seek her, and to be cold, courteous, and respectful, as befits a good secretary whenever I saw her in public or in the absence of witnesses. But finally when she called to me one afternoon: 'Come here, your lordship!' and beckoned to me with her index finger like a hook, I gave myself up for lost and no tiresome explanations were needed. We understood each other. She never succeeded in taming me, but I would be telling a lie if I were to boast of having dominated her. The truth is that I have to be on the defensive every moment, and the instant I relax, she wins a point over me.

"On the other hand," he wrote, "I have the feeling that I am losing ground nowadays. What are we coming to in the end?" He goes on to give some indelicate details regarding the relations he was maintaining with the president's wife during the periods when he was free from his official services as secretary to the president. And at last he comes to what was upsetting him so much, those cursed spiritualistic séances.

"How right I was," he exclaims, "to distrust that stupid business with the spirits! But all in vain. One always can find arguments to persuade oneself, and they will move one toward something that one nonetheless is struggling against. Specious arguments, of course, nonsense, such as: serious people would not get together there week after week just for the mummery; joining hands above the table with people like X or Z, for example, was a way of making friends; finally, what could I lose by doing it. I could kick myself for letting her talk me into it.

"During the first two or three weeks it even seemed as if the foregoing rationalizations had a certain validity. On the day of my initiation, if it may be called that, no phenomena worthy of note appeared, nothing in particular happened, and it all more or less fell flat. It added up to nothing—kid games. That fool of a woman, Mme Loreto, importuned us as usual, as always, with her everlasting yammering about an astral Presence whom she keeps pursuing in vain. Seemingly there is no way to keep her from butting in every time, interfering, calling, invoking, begging, weeping, and turning hysterical and troublesome. Some of the others used to smile with saintly patience, but the rest of them wanted to skin her alive. Concha, the Big Boss Woman, used to insult her and make her shut up, but it seems no one can stop her, even though on more than one such occasion manifestations that promised to be interesting were put to flight. That is the curse of this kind of meeting, and one and all must resign themselves.

"As I say, the first meetings I attended were nothing special. I had gone against my will, and I felt angry, annoyed, bored. For several weeks running I wasted my time on the same sort of thing, always postponing my decision not to appear at the next séance. Then suddenly last March, when I was least expecting it—bang!—I found myself in the dance. The medium had started to go into a trance, with her eyes rolled back almost as if in a swoon, and finally she began to utter nonsense addressed to your humble servant. I grew angry; I don't care for clowning.

"The late Senator Rosales was claiming to speak through her mouth, addressing his words to me—me alone, with whom he had never exchanged a word in his life—and was issuing warnings and entrusting me with a mission that . . . come, come! Why me? And what a mission! Everyone was dumbstruck. As for Concha, who was at my left, she was trembling and her hand was shaking beneath mine. But what did I care about Senator Rosales? What did he have to do with me? How could he be bothering his head over the fate of this poor cat? No, they can't take away from me what is mine, the idea! I told Concha so later when, after the séance, we met to exchange impressions in the private room of our guardian and fairy godmother, the illustrious general's widow, Doña Loreto, Malagarriga's relict. Would such messages, warnings, and other nonsense have come from Senator Lucas Rosales, no less? Then why not from Bolívar the Liberator? Didn't the Liberator Bolívar have any orders for me? Tell that to someone else!

"The Big Boss Woman's attitude turned out to be somewhat disconcerting, however, in the face of that manifestation. As usual I had gone to wait for her in Loreto's bedroom. I was standing near the dresser, turning over all that foolishness in my mind when they finally arrived together; and seeing that her friend remained discreetly in the boudoir, ready to entertain herself with her radio as usual, I called to her to come in, for I wanted to tell them both, and the whole wide world if possible, that the whole thing seemed to me simply id-i-ot-ic. But the Big Boss Woman was ready to fall apart with fear. Who would have thought it? Laughing and insolent, in her way, but half dead of fright. The trembling of her hand had been no joke, then. That was hard to believe. I fancied at first that she was trying to make light of it and was doing it as clumsily as any flustered amateur actress at a fair. I almost gave her a slap to make her stop such nonsense. But actually she was not acting: her fear was genuine and overpowering. And when I shouted at her and asked her why the hell Senator Rosales should call me, that no such a thing would ever enter any human head, she stared at me in stupefaction as if I were mad. Suddenly, taking a tone of the softest and most reasonable kindliness, in contrast to mine, she urged me: 'See here, Tadeo, you must believe me. Take the advice that has been given you, regardless of who it comes from. How can you explain the messages that come from the other world by the reasoning of this world? If the senator has spoken directly to you, he must have his reasons. Don't despise his advice. Don't be stubborn. Don't be overbold.'

"She was speaking calmly, almost sadly. I shook her by the arms, not caring about the presence of Loreto. 'But see here, stupid, how can you think? . . .' I broke off my question; I was the one to whom nothing had occurred after I had thought of it so long. I spoke to the other woman, looking for support. 'Don't you think so, Loreto?'

[180]

"Loreto turned on me a blank, fear-filled look, and did not say a word. Then Concha asked her: 'Please, Loreto, won't you leave us alone a moment, eh, dearest?' That was what her friend had been wanting. Within half a minute the rumblings, complaints, and groans of the radio could be heard coming from the other side of the door. That was the usual means of covering up our noises.

"But this time there was no question of that. With a great effort, Concha controlled her nerves and undertook the task of persuading me, giving me caresses that left me cold. And as I would not let myself be won over so easily by her usual resources, she called out the reserves, and resorted to something she could not tell me without circumlocutions. She unbosomed herself, saying that until quite recently, the matter had not gone beyond a mere ripple. She had not wanted to cause me any alarm before she was certain, but those mere glimmerings had now grown into serious signs (and I must do her the favor of recognizing that in such matters women never are mistaken). Just in case any doubt had remained, the senator's warning had come, like the voice of a soul crying out for vengeance and wanting to range himself on our side! I shouted at her: 'Go on! Cough it up once and for all, for God's sake!' She certainly coughed it up. She said that Bocanegra (you know already that he always operates by stealth) was plotting our downfall.

"Naturally that left me dumfounded. 'But why?' I asked like an imbecile. 'What do you mean, why?' She burst into her insufferable giggle and cast a glance at the bed. 'What do you think?' she asked with growing astonishment. 'Can it be possible? How?' 'How? And how!' she replied, then went on to explain at once: 'Alas, my darling! Don't you know very well that there's always someone ready to carry tales, someone who'll drop a hint?' The fool woman said that to me almost with an air of triumph, then added: 'See here, would you like me to tell you something? I've already begun to be afraid of the ambitions of that puppet, Pancho Cortina. Permit me to remind you that his is an ambition without bounds. I tell you again, there are serious signs, and I'm not fooling.'

"I can't deny that if what she had been intending to do was to rob me of my sleep, she succeeded. I never closed my eyes all night. I kept going over and belittling episodes I knew about in which Bocanegra had rid himself—treacherously, as she had said—of intimate collaborators against whom he had turned when they were most in his confidence. And as I tossed in bed, I could not get out of my mind the case of Domenech in particular, for it had fallen to me to be an exceptional witness to that, and I had played a personal part in it, furthermore—along with Pancho Cortina, to be sure, or, rather, as his acolyte—at the express orders of the Chief. 'He's a thief,' he had said, thus passing sentence during the breakfast hour, and the wealthy director of the National Bank for Credit and Subsidies supped that night in the detention prison. Domenech saved his skin, yes, but only to become an object of derision because of his downfall, and to parade his destitution through the streets, bars, and saloons of the capital until he finally managed to escape precariously across the border. Today he is working in one of the Dutch factories without making a peep. But why deceive myself? Should Concha's fears prove true, when it came to me there would be no worry over future employment. A moment before his arrest, Domenech had been totally unaware of anything, and to this date I don't know the real reason for his disgrace, even though I served as Bocanegra's pliers. If it was true that my turn had come, I would at least know full well what grounds he had to stand on this time. But what actual grounds did that silly woman have for her fears? As I lay awake, I was in despair because, idiot that I was, I had not demanded that she be explicit before we separated, tell me what the signs were that she had spoken of, the concrete facts, so that I might calibrate them for myself and form my own opinion.

"The first thing I did the next day the moment I was alone with her again was to be frank with her. Immediately, and on the following days up to today, she has passed on to me her observations in detail, her suspicions, conjectures, and the like; and if they do not act as tranquilizers, they are not unequivocal

[182]

either, nor do they breed that other kind of tranquility which, being sure of the worst, does give one after all.

"This has been an awful week. As if Concha were not normally prickly enough to deal with, now her nerves are raw and unmanageable. I can't cross her in the slightest way without her coming back at me with improprieties, rudeness, intemperance, so we would be quarreling in words while entirely aware that we ought to be coming to an agreement upon the facts. To make matters worse, she would turn very affectionate at times—mushy, to put it better—and would caress me in the way that always annoys me in such circumstances. We quarreled over that in the end, too, and what had started as a caress might end with a clawing or with blows. But we were yoked together, in any case, and we were going to have to pull together in the future.

"Even though it upset me a great deal to be in Bocanegra's presence—why deny it?—I set myself to spying on his gestures, attitudes, and glances, and I kept analyzing his terse words, twisting them this way and that to see if I could detect anything in them, but always in vain. Yet this negative result did not calm me, for I would have had to be overly innocent, knowing him as I did, to trust such outward appearances. On the other hand, it cost me no little effort to seem natural in front of him while I was plagued by so much uncertainty. What a hellish week! No sooner would it seem to me that I was irremediably lost and think my only salvation lay in fleeing before it was too late, in melting away overnight, in letting the earth swallow me up, vanishing in smoke, then I would take the opposite tack and suddenly, for no reason at all, would be filled with the mad confidence that all that was nothing but imagination, and would even think that if she was not putting on an act, she was at least deliberately exaggerating her fear in order to upset me all the more, and to get a tighter hold on me and force me to do whatever it was she had taken into her head. Again I entertained suspicions about the authenticity of the communication with Senator Rosales. At times it would strike me as an outright fake, entirely unbelievable, for when would Don Lucas have been likely to take any notice of this vile worm, even to make me an instrument of his venegeance in exchange for our salvation, as she kept arguing?

" 'This has got to be stopped; we've got to find a remedy,' she came to tell me finally, perhaps guessing that I was approaching the breaking point and could not take any more. 'What remedy?' I asked her coldly, in a tone almost of defiance. She gave me a long look and replied slowly, very slowly, not looking at me: 'Ah! That's up to you.' Then she added, 'Or perhaps you're a coward?'

"I could have strangled her then and there. Up to me? What was up to me? So when we had reached a stage at which there was no one to untangle the web she had woven, where the web would have to be cut, and where I was to let myself be hunted down like a starling, then it was up to me, was it? I saw red, and she, being no fool, could see it in my eyes. 'I must tell you,' she went on, feigning calm, 'that I couldn't do what I've been thinking of alone, and so it's up to you. Tell me, aren't you and I already united forever, in life or in death?' 'Speak up,' I said to cut her off short. And I stood waiting, with my arms folded. My words were like a disagreeable, threatening command—a little ridiculous, too, if you like.

"With what aplomb that damned woman knew how to extricate herself! Without any doubt she was convinced that my state of mind indeed had reached the saturation point, and she was determined to propose to me without any more dillydallying the way out that she had already planned. And as my attitude did not leave her much room for play, she went on to confide to me that she had spent the preceding night pondering the problem, our problem, and the only solution that she could find was to get rid of Bocanegra right away, before he could cut us off in full flight, that there was no other alternative left us, in fact. Rabies is cured when the dog is dead. After all, it was a case of dire necessity, of legitimate self-defense. In short she served me up the plan of what she most surely had every intention of carrying out, dramatized by my collaboration, had I not shown myself so refractory, so closed against her, so angry, and so hostile. She told it to me in the form of a narrative, as if a long inner debate she had carried on with herself was being put into words. Those problems of hers which she now set before me had been prepared in advance and concerned the best, surest, least dangerous way of getting rid of Bocanegra. I was well aware of all that as I followed her clever sketch, which she had been ready to come forth with and lay before me as soon as her chance should crop up in the course of a conversation with me. Like Socrates with an ignorant listener, she was hoping to get from me the result she had prefabricated in her head. And what was that marvelous result? That the best thing to do in order to eliminate the danger hanging over our heads—that is, in order to eliminate Bocanegra—was for me to drop some powders she had diligently obtained for me into his drink, so that, with alcohol to reinforce their effect, they would insure His Excellency an eternal sleep.

"As I was listening to her proposal, I was detesting her, but I kept my face as wooden as a stick. She finished and was silent then, scrutinizing me with ill-concealed anxiety. In the same tone as before, with my arms still folded, I ordered her: 'Go on!' 'Go on with what?' she screamed at me, furious. I answered her with unchanging calm: 'What comes next?'

"She was at no loss for a reply; she had that prefabricated, too. She already had thought of what would come next, even if we had no options of any kind left. Although it might entail a certain risk for us, the sudden death of the president would deflect for the time being the lightning that seemed so imminent. And once we had got ourselves out of that with whole skins, then . . . who could tell? 'It doesn't matter much to me, for myself,' she lied, 'but as for you, darling, you're a man, you're young, and you're in a position in which something, in fact a great deal, can be done to influence the course of events. After things have settled down, you could step in and exert an influence on the solution of whatever problem comes along, all the more so as you will know in advance what we are in for and when it will come. In short, God will tell you!'

[185]

visit me in my dreams. 'The real reason I appeared,' as he expressed it to me, 'was to confirm and corroborate for myself what the medium said, but not without making some corrections and some more precise and accurate statements.' Although he had manifested a brusque rudeness during the séance, the doctor proved very verbose in my dream, and quite faithful to his customary style and manner. He told me that he could understand my doubts perfectly, 'because that medium ('You, he said, 'with your unfailing perspicacity, must undoubtedly have noticed it') is what I would call a consummate coprophage, and I had a hard time speaking through her mouth. Have you noticed, Tadeo, how the use of Greek words permits cultivated people to formulate certain concepts that elude the grosser phrasings of the vulgar? Coprophagous: from *phagos,* he who eats, and *kopros,* meaning excrement. Well, that's what she is: a dung-eater. Were you able to recognize my refined speech in the rusticity, or, to be more exact, the plebeianism of her words? I'll bet you didn't. Of course you didn't. A completely inept woman. But I had no other way to make myself heard, no vehicle more appropriate, and I could not insist on the niceties, for it was very important to me to be able to communicate with you.'

"The doctor was wearing a silk handkerchief around his throat and he pulled it away with his finger and stretched his neck. I handed him my usual joke; I asked him if he was being throttled, and his eyes gleamed with irony. For the first time, I realized then that the joke was funny to him. He pretended to turn serious, however, and to chide me. 'Those jokes are in bad taste, and you ought not to crack them at the expense of a man who is worthy of your respect, understand? I'll overlook them, for I know very well you don't make them with any bad intention, and that basically you love me. But it would seem you're not very much interested in what I've come to tell you,' he added. 'Don't interrupt me again, please.'

"Interest me? He was interesting me very much; it wasn't that. I hadn't interrupted him because I was not interested, but because I was in no hurry to hear what he had to say. In any case, I felt sure of what he was about to tell me. He had already told me in substance: that he had come to confirm, *et cetera*. Consequently, each time he tried again to talk to me, I interrupted him again. Until finally he said to me, '*Au revoir*,' and stuck out his long, long tongue at me in the most comical way. My dream ended there.

"Some days one wakes up with a headache and gets up in a bad mood, out of the wrong side of the bed. After that one might say he's out of sorts for the entire day. That is what has happened to me today. I had hardly left my room, hardly drunk my wretched coffee in the office, when I began to grumble that whatever I do, say, think, try, maneuver, want, and plan in this world lacks any sense, that my existence—not this, that, or the other thing, but my very existence—is nothing but sheer folly. 'What reason should there be,' I kept asking myself between sips, 'why I, Tadeo Requena, son of the late Belén Requena, an outstanding matron in the village of San Cosme, should be here, sitting in this office in the National Palace, looking out on the parade ground, holding the job of Private Secretary to the President, handing out work to employees under me, and watching over them? Why must I keep drafts off Bocanegra and go to bed with his wife on the sly as one more of my routine tasks? For no reason. Just because. And so on, today, tomorrow, and forever. Why all that? . . .' Of course such ideas, as I know, were the effect of the bad dream, of feeling out of sorts, of nausea from the lukewarm coffee prepared by the doorman. There could be no other reason, yet I did in fact feel loathing for everything, for everyone, and for myself most of all. And as I couldn't bear myself, couldn't stand myself any longer, instead of remaining harnessed to the treadmill, I went downstairs and out into the street without a word to anyone. With no destination in mind, of course, only to see if I could not clear my head a little in that way.

"But I instantly realized that I am not accustomed to walking like that, for the simple pleasure of walking, as people usually take a walk. I hate meeting the fools who greet me or don't greet me. Besides, if that business of wandering around like an idiot, heading nowhere, constitutes a pleasure, I have forgotten it, if I ever knew it. I have forgotten it. It meant San Cosme to me, in some degree, and I have forgotten it.

"I passed in front of the Aurora and saw out of the corner of my eye that, early though it was, several idlers already were settled on the other side of the window. I debated whether or not I should enter and sit down, too. But what would I have to drink? And while I hesitated, I was going on my way and there was no point in retracing my steps. It was not worth the trouble. Besides, I was aware of an impediment within me. What do I mean by an impediment? Well, just this—something that was shackled to me, that was dragging on me, that was holding me back. Everything was so strange—those streets, those stores, the very people I was looking at, half distracted—everything.

"The memory of my first arrival in the capital buzzed into my mind like a hornet. I was in a jeep belonging to the police, with Pancho Cortina. I had passed through the city only twice (going and coming in great haste at the time of Dr. Rosales's suicide not long before, and again in an automobile), just as a fruit is cut, from the center to the outside. Now it was different; I was seeing the same film again, but in slow motion, mortally slow. I was walking, and I walked and I walked, as in a dream, as if I still was dreaming. Could I be dreaming still? Could this perhaps be another phase of the same nightmare? I was asking myself that when I suddenly felt, as I was going along at my most distracted, that someone was tugging at my arm. Well, I turned around, and whom should I see? Angelo! Yes, Angelo, his face close to mine, uttering his familiar grunts, his big idiot mouth wide open, and his smiling little eyes very tiny, like a mouse's.

"I gave a start. 'You scared me, stupid!' I scolded him. He had frightened me by pulling at me as I was walking by with my head in the clouds. I had fallen, as it were, into the middle of a market beside this unforeseeable event, next to this ridiculous Angelo. Behind his head and over his shoulder I saw delivery trucks, stalls for vegetables, for produce, for onions, for spices. The place smelled of fish, like dirty water. And I could not take my eyes off that Angelo there before me, completely wretched, all torn, dirty, disheveled, unshaved, and with his beard sprouting. He looked like a beggar. Not only did he look like it; he was a beggar. He was holding himself up by clinging tightly to my arm, and he was shaking me to and fro. He was laughing quite happily while his other hand, held open, alternately made the gesture of begging and of joining the tips of his fingers and carrying them to his mouth to signify that he was hungry. He would not let me go.

"No, it was not a dream. What a wretched idea it had been to go out for a walk without any purpose, through streets and markets where I could not find whatever I had lost! I felt as annoyed as a fly in a spider's web. I put my hand in my pocket and shoved a handful of coins into Angelo's palm as a ransom for my freedom, whereupon he pointed toward the door of a saloon facing the sidewalk straight ahead, and left me in great haste. I went on my way no less quickly, intending to return to the center of the city and take refuge in my cave again. But before I had reached the corner, I turned around to try to catch sight of him again. I don't know what impulse moved me, but the fact is that I turned around. There he was, absorbed now in inspecting what some boy was doing to the wheels of his bicycle. I went up to him. 'Angelo!' He looked at me, somewhat startled. 'Angelo, come here,' I said to him. This time it was I who took him by the arm, and he abandoned his uncomfortable, boisterous delight and suddenly turned calm. We walked on and I kept asking myself where I was going and why; actually, I did not know what to do with that feeble-minded boy. We came to a dusty little plaza and went to sit on a stone bench beneath a canopy of scruffy palm trees. 'Angelo,' I asked him, 'where are you living now? Where do you go to bed at night? Where do you sleep?' The rascal understood me all right, but he tried to make himself out more foolish than he was, with his everlasting giggle. He emitted laborious noises as if trying to answer me in his fashion, but I am convinced that he was making fun of me, putting on the effort it cost him, when the truth was that he had not the slightest notion of telling me. I was able to read all that in the depths of his little rat eyes, plus the malice of the idiot, by God! Then I began to grow angry. I grabbed him by the wrist and squeezed hard. 'Now you're going to tell me, right now, what hole you crawl into, you skink.' But he was sly enough to get it into his head to whine then, and he started to raise a rumpus by letting me know that I was hurting him. Actually I had not gone that far or anywhere near it. He stared at me with a heavy frown, grunting reproachs.

" 'Come on, Angelo!' I whispered to him, very gentle now, for the *tristitia vitae* had entered my heart at one stroke. His shrewd little eyes studied me, but I said no more. We stayed a while longer, sitting side by side on the stone bench. It was extremely hot under the heavy, rain-charged clouds, and I did not know what to do. By that time I hadn't the heart to decide anything, to think about anything. My head was aching. I would take an aspirin when I got back or if I should pass a drugstore along the way.

"A dog came near us, sniffing around, and Angelo seized the animal with remarkable quickness and showed it to me triumphantly. I felt a very unpleasant reaction at seeing how it struggled and kicked in his arms in its desperate desire to be free. 'Let it go, you louse,' I warned him. He released it and doubled up with laughter at the spectacle of its escape across the dusty square.

" 'Let's go, Angelo,' I said to him, finally. We started to walk again. I bought candy for him in a sweetshop in the quarter and gave him a little more money. 'Do you always hang around that same market, Angelo?' I asked him as I was leaving. And he answered me with repeated, overly insistent affirmative gestures: yes, yes. Who knows!"

Tadeo's memoirs break off again at this point, and now the story must remain truncated. The young secretary was not to write any more until the night when Bocanegra died and he himself was to go immediately afterward to join his Chief in the next world. But that night he still found the time, before finally quitting this one, to leave a few more pages in writing —his last.

C H A P T E R

26

++++++++++++++++++++++++++

During my conversation with Aunt Loreto, which I already have covered at some length, a small problem for a detective story still remained floating in the air, as we may recall, and by rare good luck, I hold the key to it. The problem was this: Doña Concha, the president's wife, communicates to her intimate friend and my relative that Tadeo has just assassinated Bocanegra. But the shot that is to leave us orphaned of our president is heard only *after* she has made this announcement. Wasn't that it? If I were to sit down to write that mystery novel, I would lay out a whole series of ingenious hypotheses as possible alternative solutions before making up my mind to offer the right one to the voracity of the curious reader. As we are not dealing here with more or less entertaining fiction, however, but with establishing the historical facts, I must hasten to inform the reader by means of trustworthy documents and in plain words what really took place.

I have said that I came to find it all out by a lucky happenstance. Neither I nor anyone else ever could have known the intimate details of the drama if the traitor himself had not made up his mind to consign it to writing with an eye to posterity, whose minister I have made myself. On the very night of the crime, as the dénouement of the plot was approaching, young Tadeo was scribbling alone in the silence of his office. What an incredible application to literature our conscientious secretary to the president has shown! He was diligently filling pages, which he was to leave on his desk, and which that strange chance, whose proper name I shall mention later, took it upon itself to bring to my sinful hands, together with all the rest of the manuscript I have been exploiting so heavily in the preparation of this work.

"Consummatum est!" Tadeo exclaims in beginning his final pages. Then he goes on to explain: "The thing is done now, and there's no undoing it. The reception, brilliant as usual, has ended. The guests—various dignitaries both civil and military, members of the diplomatic corps, writers, beautiful ladies and elegant gentlemen—all have gone home. Then the palace and the entire city were drowned in silence, almost at a stroke. Each in his place, his blood loaded with alcohol and weariness, all of them are asleep now, their daily troubles, tasks, and fears forgotten.

"All of them, except me. Here I am alone. I am wakeful, for I alone know how momentous tomorrow will be. Even the journalists are quietly at rest after turning over to their editors their usual honeyed reports of the reception, all unaware of the uproar, the raw sensation the next day holds in store for them. But I, who am in the know, am waiting.

"And she, too. She, too, is waiting, her eyes closed in feigned sleep at his side, until the swollen bulk of Bocanegra, in actual sleep, shall begin to thresh about in the mortal throes of the death that the loving hand of his spouse has prepared for him with such great care, and that I, his private secretary, his protegé, the man most in his confidence, have served him dissolved in his drink.

[194]

"Yes, she must feel satisfied now; what she wanted so much has been accomplished. And the whole thing proved so easy, very easy indeed—she was right about that—even too easy. Once the liquid—liquid, not powders in the end—had been poured into his goblet of rum, he himself administered successive doses to himself by signaling me with a glance, as usual, for one drink after another. And he himself announced that the dose had been more than sufficient when—also according to old custom—he began to show signs of heaviness in his eyelids, his tongue, his hand, all those well-known signals which always were obeyed by the guests like a bugle call to retreat, some of them with such diligence that they would leave without even saying good-bye to their host, considering it useless, impertinent even to make their civil *adieux* to him in that state. Those polite people never dreamed last night that they were thus passing up their final opportunity to shake hands with President Bocanegra. I, for my part, escorted him to his room like one who . . .

"Ah, if that woman could read my thoughts, she surely would be laughing at me. But can she divine them, I wonder? I fancy that I can hear her, hear her mocking tone: 'Coward!' No one can get along with her. I keep asking myself how that brute of a female can lie there next to her victim, waiting to see if the effects of the liquid are as infallible as she was promised. All right, I too did my share. I played my part, as far as that goes, and now it's up to me to wait alone. I have to stay here until she gives the agreed-upon cry of alarm to activate the spring and start the farce. But how the time drags! How slow the minutes are, how laggard the clock during the night hours!

"Chances are that they fooled her; they sold her *acqua fontis* in place of poison, and tomorrow the shouts of laughter will be Homeric. Although I doubt that. Deceive her? No. What may have happened is that she too is afraid of all that still must be done, and is granting herself a breathing spell. She has not yet nerved herself to raise the curtain. After all, no one is as strong as she pretends to be, and perhaps at this very moment she is sitting next to the corpse or standing in the doorway not daring to unleash the action she had seen to in advance with so much care. On the other hand, who knows but that Bocanegra has gone, or may go directly from his drunken stupor into the sleep of death or, in spite of what they assured her, into a cruel agony? . . ."

Here Tadeo's wanderings are cut short in the middle of a page. I am the one who added the ellipsis. It does not occur in the manuscript; that page never was finished. Conversely, another single sheet has been added later to explain to us—a curious mania under such circumstances and at such a time—all that happened as a sequel. What actually had occurred was that instead of hearing the screams agreed upon and awaited, meant to arouse the palace with a cry for help the moment she had made up her mind to disclose the supposedly sudden death of her husband, what Tadeo actually heard, what brought him out of his morose reflections, was the bell that Bocanegra had had installed on his little night table so that he could summon his secretary to his own room whenever he took the notion to. How terribly startled Tadeo was when he heard a ring from his Chief, whom he had assumed to be dead! It was like a command from beyond the grave. But he bethought himself instantly that it must be Concha, that she, not Bocanegra, must be pressing the button in there. Confident of that, he went straightaway to see what was going on.

No, that had been no literary mania of his, nor was it a puerile and callow literary preoccupation, altogether unbelievable under the circumstances. Come what might, young Requena had wanted to leave those lines behind him, for he had been suspecting that he was caught in a trap that his instincts had forewarned him of, though in vain. He had therefore set down the essential facts in his own handwriting, so that, if he should be arrested, they would serve as accusation and proof against his accomplice, and so avenge him. The timely appearance of those papers would set off a bomb at the right moment. That they should fall, as they did fall, into the hands of a man who would keep them in fear until he could pass them on to me, was something entirely unforeseeable, and to a certain degree it invalidated his calculations, correct in principle. In any case, the notes will serve at the least as testimony before the high court of History, although there is no chance at the moment that they can be used in due process in the courts of justice—things are in a fine state for such niceties! For her part, History already has avenged him without needing such testimony.

"I went to the president's bedroom on the run," Tadeo says in concluding his story. "But instead of finding Concha there, as I had fully expected—for I felt sure that it was she who had called me for some reason—I found myself face to face with Bocanegra himself, a mortal sight, half propped up in his bed. Surely my face must have turned as corpse-like as his. I stood paralyzed on the threshold. Very slowly, in a muted voice, very exhaustedly, but never taking those eyes off me, he said to me: 'She herself . . . she herself has told me everything. Did you know that? She told me just so that I could have you brought here to face me before I give up the ghost. Did you know that?' He paused to take a breath, then added hoarsely: 'But I'm not going to kill you. No. Go on living, you wretch!' He scrabbled under the pillow, scratching at the sheets with his dirty fingernails and eagerly grasped his pistol, then tossed it at me with loathing. I caught it in the air. I stared at it a moment before raising my eyes again, and immediately (I don't know how the idea even came to me—perhaps it was in order to rid myself of his stare) I squeezed off a shot at him. His head struck the wall. And then I turned toward the hallway, hoping that Concha would finally appear at the sound of the pistol shot. Where could the woman have got to?

"But she never appeared, and I am not going to look for her now. What would be the use? There's no point in that now. I am back in my office and I am leaving the news of what happened on this sheet of paper so that the essential part of this story won't be missing. After all, my shot did nothing more than hasten the death that Bocanegra already had in his body. Perhaps it spared him suffering, relieved him of his pain."

Those are the last words that Tadeo Requena ever wrote. The rest of the story, as he calls it (stories about real happenings always break off minus some essential part), is known, but only partly known, through several complementary sources. Some data were offered me, you will remember, by my Aunt Loreto. And Pancho Cortina, who could illuminate it down to the last detail of the many still lacking, if he were of a mind to do so, still is around. For example, it is known that Doña Concha had called him on the telephone, although it is not known what those two had plotted previously. It is known that he came, but left his bodyguard downstairs; it is not known why. It is known that he went upstairs to look for Tadeo. What words they exchanged are not known, if indeed any were. It is known that Tadeo actually did not think of defending himself. But perhaps he had no time to . . .

27

++++++++++++++++++++++++++++

And now the time has come for me to reveal
who it was that handed over to me that manuscript by Tadeo
Requena, the king piece of the present history. That was
Sobrarbe, the administration officer who worked under the immediate orders of Requena in the office of the Private Secretary
to the President. Sobrarbe, only Sobrarbe, and there is no mystery
whatever about it, as we shall see in the next few pages.

Although the circumstances of domestic and private arrangements are of little importance in themselves, it will help at this
point to explain that Sobrarbe boarded at the *pension* in which
I have been living for goodness knows how long. That was the
Fairy Lady Pension (and let it be said in passing that the name
would attract Sobrarbe)—a house that was respectable, more than
acceptable really to those who lodged there regularly, and which
has suited me for more reasons than one. In the first place, I
have a room on the ground floor here, contiguous to the dining

room, which is convenient for me, almost necessary, given my physical requirements, with my wheelchair and other impedimenta. Then, too, it is centrally situated, a few steps from the Aurora Café; and best of all, they have been considerate in their price in view of my long stay and do not bother me when I occasionally fall behind in my rent.

Sobrarbe, a bachelor *et pour cause* (a reason quite different from mine) also has been one of the guests from time immemorial. In spite of that, however, our relations never have gone beyond the customary civil good-days and good-nights, and a very occasional longer conversation (which, of course, does not hamper us in our alertness to our own lives and our respective miracles). In the dangerous times we are living through nowadays, the formalities are more often set aside. Distances are narrowed, and people approach one another more often, for good or ill, and this has happened with Sobrarbe. When he learned that I maintain frequent contact—rumor, which I never deny, tends to characterize the contact as intimate—with Old Olóriz, whose unspecified importance and influence in present-day politics is sure to be bruited about—then and not before, Sobrarbe came to me to unburden himself of the question of the manuscript.

Of course I seized upon it with delight, trying not to make my surprise or my interest too transparent. All the same, I'm a fine one for anybody to tell his fairy tales to, forsooth! But after all, Sobrarbe is an innocent, and it was not at all hard for me to make him spit out what was sticking in his craw. It came down to this: that upon finding scattered over his boss's (Tadeo's) desk, and of course reading, the pages written at the last moment by Tadeo, he decided that in view of their astonishing content and the general context of the situation, he ought to confiscate those compromising papers and at the same time take possession of the bunch of notes which he soon found in the drawer.

He had gone to work as buoyantly, cheerfully, happily and contentedly as on any other morning, and though he had noticed something unusual as he crossed the patio, he had not found out all that had happened until he went upstairs and heard it from the lips of a doorman in all its enormous seriousness. What he was told was that during the small hours of the morning, Señor Requena had shot His Excellency in his bed—by his malicious glance, Sobrarbe underlined the inferences that could be drawn from the time and place. After that, Colonel Cortina, who had dropped down on the scene like rain from the skies, had fired his gun at the assassin and riddled him with bullets (the bloodstains still were visible). So there were two dead bodies in the building at that very moment—almost three, for Colonel Cortina had fractured his skull when he fell down the staircase and had had to be carted off unconscious for emergency treatment.

"You can just imagine, Señor Pinedo, the confusion that reigned in the palace. But it's hard to believe! When I say confusion, I don't mean to imply any uproar, or shouting, or running back and forth. Not at all. It was more like a mortal confusion, a kind of stupefaction, a disorder and panic that showed up in a negative way, in complete silence, immense wariness, concealment. The president's wife herself doesn't seem to know what she's doing, as is only natural after such a great loss, poor lady. Then I," Sobrarbe went on, "grabbed the telephone as a newborn calf seizes the maternal udder and notified my two office co-workers. I impressed upon them what had happened and told them not to come to work unless they wanted to, because things were bound to turn out to be somewhat strong for their delicate nerves. Of course, they came; their curiosity was stronger. But meanwhile I had inspected the desk of my recently extinguished superior in rank, not out of curiosity, but from a sense of duty, and, Señor Pinedo, I almost dropped dead, I swear it, when I read . . . Well, as I though of that barbarous deed, I quickly went and hid to read those pages. And then I went to work searching the drawers and pigeonholes in his desk (without having to force the locks, as the key was there) until finally I came upon this stack of papers, which that industrious little ant was forever working on, but never letting me get a peep at, and I decided that it was up to me to safeguard them . . ."

"Along with the rest of Tadeo's little souvenirs," I finished, with a smile.

Certainly I was not expecting my shot to have such a resounding effect. Sobrarbe blushed, the unwary man, up to his very eyebrows, and cast a glance full of fear at me, like a pickpocket caught red-handed. For a moment he was silent, not knowing what to say for himself. Then he returned my knowing little laugh with a false and guilty one. But he was very quick to wriggle out of my clutches! Willy-nilly he came out with his rascality; he had to confess it to me, half stammering. Among other things of little worth, Requena had been keeping a certain sum of money, a considerable amount, in his office inside a handsome little strongbox. Probably it represented his savings (why shouldn't he have saved almost his entire salary, seeing what a monk's life he had led, like a hermit in the palace, and with all found, too?), and the wretch had kept it there in bills, piled one on top of another. With praiseworthy speed Sobrarbe had appointed himself general legatee, sole beneficiary of that sum. But now he seemed disposed to transfer it to me with touching disinterestedness, together with the manuscripts. He had kept it all only for reasons of elementary safety and with the intention of preventing anyone from stealing it. He would therefore bow to my judgment; he would let me decide. After all, Requena had no relatives, not even any friends, it seemed, so . . .

After such a general confession, I granted Sobrarbe a plenary indulgence. Having things like that in his possession would compromise him—the manuscripts I mean. As for the money, it was difficult to identify by its very nature, especially if handled with prudence, so that we could always find a solution appropriate to the circumstances of the case and the times. The important thing at the moment was the papers. He was more than pleased to hand them over to me, and I suppose, I hope, that he understood how greatly it would behoove him to be discreet, though with people of that stripe one can never be sure.

28

++++++++++++++++++++++++++++

What role does the factor of chance play in history? Here is a theme ripe for an academic dissertation, matter for a doctoral thesis by a candidate in philosophy and literature. The question of the role attributed to Cleopatra's nose could be posed immediately, of the concept of fortune in the Renaissance, and of the mysterious *quid* that we call luck in everyone's daily life—his good or bad luck—and, say what you will as to whether or not it exists, it does exist indeed!

But this would be a better subject for philosophers of history than for a modest historian. The historian collates events as he finds them and presses on. As to what has some sort of influence over the general course of events, I can see no need to get involved in an attempt to determine whether it may be imputed to God or the Devil. Whether luck, chance, or perhaps the unconscious, which is blamed for everything today, may have wanted to do him a bad turn, the truth is that the fall of our elegant little colonel, who tumbled down the stairs after having written off Tadeo, did play a very decisive part in the history of our country. The historian would be justified by the fact of that broken head in permitting himself a more or less lyrical, elegiac paragraph on the subject of blind luck, or the inscrutable designs of Divine Providence if you like, for this is a matter of taste. Be that as it may, the fact—and I am sticking to the facts—is that this accident deserves the designation of fatal. Regardless of whether Pancho Cortina was an accomplice to the intrigues of the First Lady, who could say him nay, given the position to which he then had attained, and with all the forces of public order in his fist, plus the added prestige now of having been avenging angel to the president? Even granting that he may not have been involved in any machinations, he was by all odds the undisputed arbiter of the situation and had every assurance of becoming Bocanegra's successor as head of the state.

But it happened that, after exterminating the traitor Requena with his death ray, our hero was running downstairs, happily chasing what he doubtless considered his unmistakable and brilliant destiny, when his very haste caused him to fall on his head. He slid, he rolled . . . and on the later day when he came to after his brain injury, it was only to find himself in a hospital bed or, more accurately, in the little infirmary of the military prison, where—with all the honors and considerations owing to his rank, to be sure—he was being held incommunicado for disposition by his superiors.

For disposition by his superiors? What did that mean? In the beginning he knew nothing, of course. How could he know anything? He would never have dreamed that, while he was floating in limbo, a *junta* for the Defense of the People had been constituted, made up of delegations from the ranks of the army, and that, the supreme command had just been taken over, in great haste, by a triumvirate of sergeants representing the armed forces. That one of them should be his own subordinate, Sergeant Major Falo Alberto, from the first squadron of the mounted police, was doubtless something that gave Pancho Cortina cause to squirm among his sheets and bandages.

Although these events are astonishing, they are not ultimately obscure—not in their genesis, their manifestations, or their proceedings. The historian possesses all the data, so that when the time comes, he can organize them within a congruent and clear relation, from the stormy session of the cabinet, which had met spontaneously at the palace when the news came of Bocanegra's assassination, to the present moment. The dispute that broke out in that emergency cabinet meeting and ended in insults, blows, and fistfights among the members of the government was an outgrowth of the always latent rivalry among the Under-Secretaries of Infantry and Aviation, as were all the indescribable scandal, the more or less open threats and armed conflict; the archbishop's efforts at mediation, as he maneuvered to turn the waters back to their source or—as the malicious versions had it —to turn them into his watermill; the acts of violence that began to emerge sporadically; the insubordination in the barracks accompanied by the incredible spectacle of confusion and impotence among the officers' corps; and, finally, the proclamation of a state of war by decree from the directorate, or triumvirate, whom the ranks had placed at the head of their famous *junta* for the Defense of the People.

That was what Pancho Cortina awakened to: being arrested and held incommunicado at the disposal of that Falo Alberto and two completely unknown sergeants, Tacho Salmagundi and the Beast. So, my colonel, form your scar tissue with patience! And above all, my boy, don't make a move! In your condition that would be dangerous.

CHAPTER

29

++++++++++++++++++++++++++

As Pancho Cortina is not a very patient man, he is not likely to stay quiet very long, especially as there must be an accounting of the situation we have come to, and as all those who are entertaining in some measure a reasonable hope—and while there is life there is hope—must be added up, even if only to exclude them from the final figure, which is promising, threatening, or fearful, depending on the point of view. But is very much choice left? Well, then, in the course of my conversation with Loreto . . .

Half the account of that conversation was left untold back there, but I am not going to return to it now, for this would become a story without an end. Besides, as I skim over my writing, I notice that I have not managed after all to foreshadow the ending with any fidelity. Perhaps I could not achieve that no matter how hard I tried. Among the infinite number of items let fall by the good lady as she chattered away in her feeble-minded fashion, as insubstantial and spineless as her nature, I was always and inevitably selecting only what has some point in relation to my peculiar interest. The result is that my aunt-in-law might seem—though she is not—a relatively shrewd person, and her judgments might carry more weight than she is capable of giving them. For this reason, perhaps it would be best for me to confine myself to extracting the meat of my soundings, verifications, or investigations as a historian and to omit the vague words they came wrapped in. After all, what I am doing here is nothing more than collecting data to serve as a foundation upon which I shall later be able to build the historical edifice I have in mind.

I shall, therefore, retain and set down in abbreviated form what will serve my purpose, and particularly what has to do with the people who have played, are playing, and perhaps will play star roles in the tragedy of our country. I am referring now to Pancho Cortina and to Old Olóriz in particular.

Doña Loreto's attitude to Cortina is almost entirely negative and adds up to antipathy. Why? Well, unless I am quite mistaken, she took it from my Uncle Antenor, who must have made abundantly clear—he was so transparent—some feeling of jealousy and spite—quite justified, naturally—over the too rapid rise of that young parvenu. It would seem that married couples, even those who do not see eye to eye on other matters or care about them, can scent things like that instantly. They will then take a stand very quickly, often a very extreme and indiscreet one. And when that happens, wives who otherwise are alienated from or even hostile to their husbands can establish a close solidarity with them which is astonishing. I cannot say that this was the case between Loreto and my Uncle Antenor, but why does she detest Cortina so heartily? As I say, the spite and jealousy of the deceased were fully justified, but neither his character nor his imagination were strong enough to anticipate the troubles he was spared by his opportune death. Actually one of those troubles, and no small one, was what led to his death. The memoirs of Tadeo illuminate the matter, for it is through them that we learn of the enormous disappointment caused my poor uncle by Bocanegra when the president, with an inde-scribable lack of consideration, decreed the promotion of his favorite lackey without even taking the trouble to notify the man who was, after all, Minister of War.

Antenor exploded out of sheer temper, as they say. And if he had not departed this dog's life in time, worse would have awaited him. We have seen that General Malagarriga hardly had passed on before Bocanegra apportioned his cabinet post among three independent under-secretaries instead of replacing him in the War Office. All three were colonels in their respective branch of the service. Then Bocanegra created still another un-der-secretaryship, also independent: the Under-Secretaryship of Public Order—for Pancho Cortina. Who could fail to notice the paths events were taking? I am not suggesting, even for a mo-ment, that Loreto realized all that, but women have a very keen nose for all phases of personal rivalry in every procedure, and Antenor's worries would have been reason enough for her to decide to loathe Pancho without knowing precisely why.

"As for Pancho, I am almost sure, Aunt Loreto, that Doña Concha had him plotting with her in her conch shell in some way that, the chances are, you don't even know about. That telephone call in half-veiled words—now, isn't that pretty sus-picious? Then, too, it's a very strange thing that Tadeo's shot was heard *after* she had told you about the assassination. Well, I wouldn't care to make any rash judgments, but I wouldn't like to have put my hand in the fire either. Who knows but that this unfortunate lady, terrified, perhaps, by the messages from beyond the grave, herself set the trap into which everyone fell, one after another, even . . ." I made the suggestion so as to stir up her animosity and her vanity and thus encourage her to talk.

She did not reject my suggestion outright, but she was visibly offended by my supposition that she could have been left in the dark about anything, and so much the more offended to have to admit . . . Finally the little wrinkles around her smeared mouth traced a grimace of retrospective reproach for her in-timate friend.

"Concha was a terror," she acknowledged. But I could not get another word out of her, perhaps because she already had blurted out the best part of what she had to say.

As a final recourse I asked her very plainly: "See here, my theory is that Doña Concha—and I repeat that her wits must have been addled by the fright the spirits had implanted in her —had made up her mind to write off her husband and her lover at the same time, Bocanegra and Tadeo both, out of sheer desperation. And I say that she had established a state of carnal knowledge for that purpose with Pancho Cortina, who is beyond redemption, just so that he could sound the alarm and make off with the spoils and leave her at least a share of the alms. What do you think, Aunt Loreto?"

Loreto stared at me wide-eyed, then shook her head. Such a thing had not entered her mind. Well, what was the point in insisting? I went on: "So if the devil had not happened by sheer chance to get tangled up in his own tail—in other words if Pancho had not fallen downstairs and broken his crown—the chances are he would be Mr. First Lady of the Republic right now."

I shot her a glance, watching for her reaction, but the reaction was nil. So, instead of mentioning, as I had thought of doing, the rumor already current—even Sobrarbe knew of it—that one of the triumvirs, Sergeant Falo Alberto, had sent a wire to his former chief, still in the hospital, and that they were exchanging messages and holding secret conclaves, I let it go and went on: "Perhaps we would have a dictator in place of the *junta* that is in charge of us today." Then I added: "It's better as it is, isn't it, Aunt Loreto? For us. There's always a chance that the members of the triumvirate may learn to listen to people with brains and experience, like our Señor Olóriz, for instance."

She smiled. We had got to the heart of the matter now. At the beginning of my visit I had taken great pains to point out to her that Old Olóriz had been the man who gave me her present address or, rather, her telephone number. Now I assumed a meditative air and reflected gloomily: "What turns life takes sometimes, what peculiar ones! To think that a man can reach the Biblical age without circumstances ever offering him a real opportunity, that he can go through his whole life just getting by, never being able to display his magnificent native talents, only to have a power as boundless as that which Señor Olóriz now holds fall suddenly and untimely into his hands later!"

My reflection was not something improvised or deceitful, aside from the peculiar modulation one adopts to impress his thoughts on the attention of the person to whom he is speaking. I was sincere. It is true that no one knows, no one ever knows anything, either about other people or about himself. Given such and such a set of circumstances, anyone is capable of surprising someone else as surely as the morning star will rise. Who would have thought that Señor Olóriz, that dirty old man, that venerable dotard, would be in a position some day to amuse himself by playing like that with other people's fate from his valetudinarian's armchair? At the risk of bearing down on the theme of luck —his, someone else's, anybody else's—I believe that if Pancho Cortina had not had the notion to fall downstairs his toothpaste smile would be gleaming in the frames of the official portraits right now, in place of the black stare of Bocanegra, which still hangs, *pro tem.*, on the façade of many public offices, though it has disappeared almost completely from the markets, stores, and bars. And Old Olóriz would continue his shady work there in the depths of his house, just as I had known him to do in the past, and as each of the Three Orangutans now composing the directory or triumvirate also knew him to do. Meanwhile, he was rubbing his hands with glee and guile, more than pleased to be meddling in that boiling subterranean province of the Special and Reserve Services, his source of money and other less tangible benefits. But when all is said and done, he was insignificant, a nugatory soothing syrup of a man, whom many despise—picturesque, somewhat irritating, but nothing more.

Yet, this is the terrible man upon whose toothless mouth, upon whose slack lips, upon whose trembling tongue, upon whose clouded brain the fate of us all now hangs!

I still was waiting for his niece, my Aunt Loreto, whose influence in the early days of the regime had settled him into a position that was to prove so strategic for him, to offer some tidbit to my voracious historian's curiosity, some prime cause, even some retrospective flourish that would throw light on the fact of his tardy and unforeseen vocation for power. But she did not choose to do so. She remained reticent.

"I can't see that his power is so great, Pinedo," she replied ingenuously to the ponderous reflections I had offered her.

Was she playing the fool? Or could it have been that not even she could measure the magnitude of the sinister influence stealthily exerted by her relative? The chances were that if a question like that were asked him to his face, he would act surprised. What power? To be sure, he had helped those novice governors of the people with some advice that they considered to be worth more than it was. Chance had decreed that they should be old "clients" of his, and they trusted him, recognizing in him an authority that could be attributed solely to his many years. And later, after the first days following Bocanegra's death had gone by, as the disorder of the revolution covered over, nourished, and put an honest face on the satisfaction of the most urgent grudges, as violence invaded the highways of custom, what was so strange about the conversion of his office into a general head-quarters for organized murder by virtue of old habit? If function can create an organ, the organ can also create a function.

As for the rest of it, the old man never had abandoned the reticent posture of a decrepit sphinx; he never had taken it upon himself to issue orders. The secret of his art resides in that very fact. Perhaps all that famous advice of his had never gone beyond the ambiguous and malevolent hint, either. I don't know. But I do know very well that in this other specific matter of the public security, on the other hand, he had lain in wait like a ferret in his hole for anyone who came looking for him, in order to lure names from his visitor, to suck suggestions from him. But only after he had been begged to would he venture to suggest how prudent it might be, in such delicate circumstances as the present ones, to keep an eye on John Doe or Richard Roe. That was enough to insure that by the following morning John

CHAPTER

30

++++++++++++++++++++++++++++++

Alas for me! Alas for my plans, for my glory as a historian! Poor Pinedito! What vain illusions you were cherishing! What grounds did you have for them? A castle of cards, and now it all topples to the ground. It is all over. Say good-bye. There is no other way out.

Even though I have been living surrounded by so many horrors, the dangers that threatened me were more or less vague until today. Then, too, in normal times, one lives tranquilly even though he knows that death awaits him, perhaps just around the corner. But everything is different now. Now I know the site of my cancer, what pistol is pointing at me. Old Olóriz showed me that by surprise. Suddenly, as I was preparing to say good-bye to him after a long conversation during which he had seemed to me especially affable and correspondingly much interested in my opinions and news, he let fall as though attaching no importance whatever to his words: "Listen, Pinedo, tell

sleeping streets, I was rolling along very happily. My grand-
mother used to say to me: "Early to bed, early to rise, makes a
man healthy, wealthy, and wise . . ." I'm safe now.

You're a great man, Pinedito! In a few hours, when the news
breaks that Old Olóriz was found strangled on the terrace of his
house at sunrise, the city and the entire country will breathe a
sigh of relief. But for the time being no one will even suspect
whose beneficent and liberating hand belled the cat. No one will
know the name of the deserving citizen to whom a grateful nation
ought someday to erect a statue.